LEVI'S WILLFUL DAUGHTER

*To Virginia,
Best wishes from an
old friend,
Oralee*

LEVI'S WILLFUL DAUGHTER

Onalee Efrusy

Copyright © 2000 by Onalee Efrusy.

Library of Congress Number: 00-191328
ISBN #:   Hardcover   0-7388-2582-4
                Softcover   0-7388-2583-2

All rights reserved. No part of this book may be reproduced or transmitted in any form or by any means, electronic or mechanical, including photocopying, recording, or by any information storage and retrieval system, without permission in writing from the copyright owner.

This is a work of fiction. Names, characters, places and incidents either are the product of the author's imagination or are used fictitiously, and any resemblance to any actual persons, living or dead, events, or locales is entirely coincidental.

This book was printed in the United States of America.

To order additional copies of this book, contact:
Xlibris Corporation
1-888-7-XLIBRIS
www.Xlibris.com
Orders@Xlibris.com

CONTENTS

PROLOGUE
August 1923 9

CHAPTER ONE
November 1887 13
CHAPTER TWO 18
CHAPTER THREE
Winter of 1888 25
CHAPTER FOUR
Spring of 1888 31
CHAPTER FIVE
Summer 1888 36
CHAPTER SIX
February 1889 41
CHAPTER SEVEN
August 1894 45
CHAPTER EIGHT
October 1898 50
CHAPTER NINE 56
CHAPTER TEN 61
CHAPTER ELEVEN
March 1899 67
CHAPTER TWELVE 74
CHAPTER THIRTEEN
Spring 1904 78
CHAPTER FOURTEEN 84
CHAPTER FIFTEEN 89
CHAPTER SIXTEEN 97

CHAPTER SEVENTEEN 104
CHAPTER EIGHTEEN 113
CHAPTER NINETEEN 117
CHAPTER TWENTY 121
CHAPTER TWENTY-ONE 126
CHAPTER TWENTY-TWO 130
CHAPTER TWENTY-THREE 134
CHAPTER TWENTY-FOUR 139
CHAPTER TWENTY-FIVE 150
CHAPTER TWENTY-SIX 156
CHAPTER TWENTY-SEVEN 162
CHAPTER TWENTY-EIGHT 166
CHAPTER TWENTY-NINE
   (Ten years later 1923) 170
CHAPTER THIRTY 174
CHAPTER THIRTY-ONE 180

*In memory of my father Carl
who's colorful stories
inspired me to write this novel.*

PROLOGUE

August 1923

Carl slowly stepped down from the train. Small puffs of smoke rose from the engine into a cloudless sky. The tracks shimmered in the August heat. Setting his valise on the platform he removed his suitcoat. It had been a long ride and his shoulders ached from sitting up straight all night. His shirt stuck to his back and the high collar rubbed his neck leaving a red mark. Taking off his straw skimmer, he wiped his face with his handkerchief. He stood for a time looking at the lush green hillside that rose up behind the railroad station. It was his destination, but it could wait. He checked his bag with the stationmaster and started down the well-worn path towards town. It seemed nothing had changed in ten years. Not the red brick front of the Wolverine Mercantile Bank or the faded white of the General Store.

Carl stopped in at both, asking the question. "Had anyone seen Levi Wakeford?" He got the same answer. No one had seen his father for several months. Mr. Allen at the bank, recalled him coming in last spring to make a deposit, but not since.

He also stopped at Cromwell's Feed and Hardware store and checked with Miss Purdy who ran the post office from the back of the store.

"Haven't seen your Pa for some time," she said peering over her wire rimmed glasses, "I've been keeping his mail for him, though." She held up a packet of letters.

Carl looked through them and recognized his own square handwriting on several. It explained why his father hadn't answered his letters inviting him to stay in Detroit with him and his family. Where was he? Carl sighed. He couldn't think of anywhere else to ask. It was time he went to the cabin. He adjusted his straw hat and started back toward the train station. His long strides quickly took him to the dirt road leading up the hill behind the tracks. He paused at the iron bridge over the Sturgeon River and gazed down at the swiftly rushing, deep blue water. Moving on, he searched the roadside and soon found an overgrown path to the left leading into the woods. He pushed aside the waist high ferns and started climbing.

The path rose steeply but it was cooler in the shade of the tall Pine trees. Crows called to one another from the high above and tree toads chirped. Thistles clung to Carl's pantlegs as he brushed aside the tangle of undergrowth that obscured the path.

He had been climbing for a half hour when he caught a glimpse of the log cabin some hundred yards ahead. An icy shiver ran through him. How could this be? He was sweating profusely and yet he felt a definite chill. Carl stopped, peering into the thick trees. He could see nothing but patches of sunlight changing the shades of green as it filtered down from above. Somewhere to the left he heard the scurrying of a small animal and the buzz of insects. Shaking off his feeling of foreboding, he hurried on.

As he approached the cabin he could see no signs of life around the small structure. Vines crawled up through the cracks in the small wooden porch. He cupped his hands and peered in the dust covered windows. The room was empty. He tried the latch on the oaken door. To his surprise, he found it unlocked. Cautiously, Carl stepped into the one room cabin.

His eyes slowly adjusted to the dim light. He noted the iron cot neatly made with a patchwork quilt. In the center of the room sat a sturdy oak table covered by faded oilcloth. A cup, spoon and bowl sat waiting. Against the far wall stood a small cook stove with an enamel coffee pot, an iron skillet and a small pan with the remains of dried oatmeal the mice had found.

Carl frowned. Wherever his father had gone, he'd left in a

hurry. Then he saw it. Levi's Bible lay on a small table next to the kerosene lamp. His spectacles folded on top.

With increasing uneasiness he returned to the small porch and sat down on the worn step. His father was an independent man and often took off to parts unknown but *never* did he leave without his bible.

The only place left to check was a small outhouse. When it proved to be empty, there was no point in staying and Carl started back down the path.

As he approached the same spot in the woods, there it was again, the strange chill. He stopped, listening. Somewhere to his right he could hear insects and the running of small feet near a large pine. He stepped off the path to investigate. As he neared the tree, his foot caught on something. He looked down to see worn boot protruding from a pile of rags. Carl pushed away the ferns and was met with a horrible stench.

He stumbled back, paling with realization. Small animals had done their job well. The familiar thatch of white hair protruding from the skull told the story. Carl staggered back to the cabin and dropped to the porch, his head reeling. Absently he picked up a piece of white cloth wedged by the step. He worried it in his hands, thinking of his father. Levi was a stubborn man, refusing to live with any of his children. What had happened here? He'd made enemies over the years with his uncontrollable anger. Had one of them taken revenge?

Looking down at the scrap of cloth he smoothed on his knee he frowned with realization. It was not a rag but a linen handkerchief with the letter "*B*" embroidered in the corner. Beatrice's? When had she been here? But more disturbing, were the dried blood stains on the delicate cloth.

Carl could control his grief no longer. He buried his face in his hands and wept.

CHAPTER ONE

November 1887

The Northern Michigan dusk fell swiftly in November. Levi Wakeford's long strides took him quickly across the clearing. Entering the woods, his hand automatically tightened on his twelve gauge shotgun. His pace slowed as he ducked his head to miss low hanging branches. He remembered one time he had been foolish enough to walk through the thick forest without carrying a weapon. A piercing scream had been his only warning when a furry body plummeted down on his shoulders. Only his thick woolen jacket had prevented the razor-like claws from reaching the bone. He recalled his rage when he had pulled the shrieking animal from his back, threw it to the ground and killed the Lynx with a well aimed kick. The encounter had given him new respect for the woods and the creatures that lived there.

As he approached a clearing he found the hollow tree he had used before. He carefully stowed his gun inside. Foolhardy or not, he did not intend to go courtin' with a firearm. It just wasn't proper. A small farm nestled in the clearing. He could barely make out the barn and outbuildings. Lights glowed warmly from the farmhouse and grey smoke curled in a spiral from the chimney. His cheeks tingled from the sting of the crisp winds that carried his breath from his lips in white wisps. There was a smell of snow in the air. His strides quickened.

Inside the farmhouse, Jenny LaBlanc, the eldest daughter of George and Josephine, was putting the supper dishes away. Her two younger sisters, Marie and Dehlia were teasing her.

"Jenny's got a boy friend." Marie chanted dancing around the warm kitchen, her thick braids flying.

"I bet he tries to hold her hand." Lucia chimed in backing away from her sister's dishtowel snap.

"Children should be seen, not heard." Jenny said.

"Girls!" came their mother's voice, speaking in french. "Take your homework upstairs, now." Lucia scooped up the McGuffy readers while Marie lit the kerosene lamp with a wooden match. As they made their way up the narrow staircase to the loft, Jenny could hear them whispering. "Bet he tries to kiss her." This was followed by giggles. Her cheeks glowed with the thought.

In the parlor, Mrs. LaBlanc, a small, plump woman, sat in a pine rocker knitting from a ball of grey yarn. George LaBlanc, a short, sturdy man with gnarled farmer's hands, whittled with even strokes on a piece of Oak forming a chair leg.

A light tap on the kitchen door made Jenny's heart race. She was glad her sisters were not there to see the telltale flush.

She patted her thick auburn hair and smoothing a few curly strands back from her face, opened the door.

"Evenin', Miss Jenny." Levi said, stooping to enter the low door frame.

"Let me take your coat." she said and turned away to hang it on a peg by the door.

"Miz LaBlanc, George," Levi nodded to her parents from the parlor door. Her mother looked up and smiled. Her father glared over the tops of his spectacles and grunted.

"Would you like some coffee, Levi?" Jenny asked, inviting him back into the kitchen.

"I surely would," he said. Following her to the table, he sat down, curling his long legs under it.

She took a heavy mug from the cupboard and poured thick black coffee from a large pot on the cook stove. She took fresh cream from a white jug, scooped in two generous spoons of sugar, the way she knew he liked it, and set it before him.

Looking over the rim of the cup, Levi took a deep swallow. His eyes took in the way the light from the lamp made Jenny's hair shine like copper. He gazed longingly at her creamy complexion and featherlike brows. When she lifted her thick lashes and searched his face with her deep brown eyes, his breath caught.

Levi's huge, rough hand moved to enclose her small one. He felt the slight tremble and smiled.

"I've come to tell you I've signed up with Claude Devereau for the winter." he said. His piercing blue eyes noted her displeasure.

Devereau's logging camp was located twenty-five miles to the north. He had been hoping to find work closer for the winter. They both knew if he went there, the chances of them seeing each other before spring were very slim.

"Devereau will pay good money for using my team," He urged gently. "Come spring I should have enough money put aside for a homestead for us."

Jenny's heart skipped a beat. "For us, Levi?"

"Course, it's for us," he smiled at the flush on her cheeks. "How can we get hitched without a homestead?"

Jenny blinked back tears. Her love for him overwhelmed her. She had wanted to marry Levi since she'd first laid eyes on this tall rugged man with the bluest eyes she had ever seen.

Heads close together they made plans. Levi would apply for a land grant in the spring and as soon as he could clear a spot for a cabin he would build one and they would be married.

They were interrupted by a cold gust of wind as the door banged open. Jenny's brother Frank came stomping in from his chores. "You here again, Levi?" his eyes noted their tightly locked hands. "What are you goin' to do all winter when you're off loggin'? You'll be some sorry sight come spring." Frank's laugh filled the room.

"You want some coffee?" Jenny withdrew her hand and started for the stove.

"He'll want something in it for the cold," her father's voice called from the parlor. "Get out the jug."

Frank heartily agreed and reached in the cupboard. He poured a generous portion of Apple-jack into his coffee. Taking a big swallow, he coughed but smacked his lips. "How about you, Levi?" he held out the jug, "Something to keep you warm besides my sister."

"Not tonight, thanks," Levi declined, fixing him with a cold stare,. "Have to be leaving," He pulled his long legs from under the table and rose.

George came into the kitchen to join Frank. Levi, standing a full head taller than the two men, seemed to fill the room, his head almost touched the ceiling. Jenny took his coat and hat from the peg and handed them to him. While he was buttoning his coat she also took down a shawl and fastened it about her shoulders.

"Where you goin', girl?" George asked setting the jug down.

"Just to the end of the path, Papa," She moved quickly to follow Levi out. "I'll be right back."

"You best keep an eye on them, Pa," Frank warned, slurping his mug to savor the last drops.

"I plan to," George said, tipping the jug over his shoulder for a long swallow. "Don't trust a man that won't take a sociable drink on a cold night."

"Damn fool," Frank muttered, "Don't even have sense enough to carry his gun in the woods."

In the dark Jenny ran to Levi's waiting arms. He crushed her small body hungrily to him. She stood on tiptoe and he bent to reach her waiting lips.

"Oh Levi, I can't wait to be your wife." she clung tightly to him. "But what about Papa?"

"Never you mind, Jen," he assured her, "Leave your Pa to me." His lips sought her willing ones again.

A patch of light stretched out from the door and Frank's silhouette filled it. "Jenny! Pa says for you to get back in her, now!" his voice called out.

They clung together for another precious moment then Levi gently withdrew his arms. "You best go." he said hishand touching her face as if to keep her image in his finger tips. "I'll try to get back before Christmas. With one last loving look he turned and was gone in the darkness.

From the edge of the forest Levi watched her small figure run to the house. He hurried to the hollow tree where he retrieved his gun, lit a small lantern and made his way through the woods.

His thoughts were racing ahead of him. He'd save all his money he'd earn working for Devereau and come spring, as soon as the roads were clear, he would head for Cheboygan and apply for a land grant. He'd heard there was some good plots over by the Pigeon river. Once he had his property he would build a cabin. Jenny's father couldn't object to a man who owned his own land.

He made his way swiftly through the woods and soon was on the road to Afton. In his mind he pictured the farm he planned to have. He would work the land and soon there would be great fields of corn and oats and a garden for Jenny. When he thought of her, the life they would share, the family they'd have, his eyes blurred with tears of joy.

Levi never thought he could feel such love. It seemed he'd always been alone. Orphaned at an early age he'd lived with various relatives but never had he felt he was part of a family. He'd managed well enough on his own. It had never mattered until he'd met this beautiful girl with gold red hair and soft brown eyes.

The moment he set eyes on her, he knew he meant to have her. The surprising thing was that she wanted him too. He couldn't believe his good fortune.

CHAPTER TWO

Levi's team of Bays was a great source of pride to him. Star and Robin were a perfectly matched pair except for the white marking on Star's forehead. They were also his means of livelihood. They were big, strong animals, standing sixteen hands. He paid the blacksmith to keep them in his barn but he took care of them personally. He brushed their shiny flanks until they shone. Levi made extra money delivering supplies between the towns of Afton, Wolverine and Black Lake. When he needed only one horse to pull a rig or wagon he chose the even tempered Star.

Levi had a small room over the Livery stable. On those rare occasions when his finances were low he sometimes went without a meal but he saw to it that his horses were always fed properly.

The next morning he settled up with Homer Clews, the blacksmith and gathered up his personal belongings. His meager possessions consisted of an extra wool shirt, two pairs of thick socks, his straight razor and his bible. He placed everything in a gunny sack. He climbed up on Star with Robin tethered behind and set off for Claude Devereau's logging camp. He reached the camp in late afternoon. It was a bustling hub of activity. The bunkhouse, a long one story building made of rough hewn logs stood in the center. To the left stood a smaller building. It appeared to be the cookhouse and mess hall.

The sound of axes rang in the air as a barn was being constructed near the edge of the forest. Stacks of marsh hay were piled in readiness to feel the stock, come winter.

A small but powerfully built lumberjack in a red plaid shirt with a wool cap jauntily sitting on the back of his head was splitting logs. He stopped his work and smiled broadly at Levi showing broken teeth and one of the largest noses Levi had ever seen.

"By Gar, tha's some fine looking team you got, my fran'" he said, His English laced with French.

The horses tossed their black manes and stamped restlessly. It had been a long trip and they were ready to be fed and watered. Levi accepted the compliment with a nod. "Can you tell me where I might put them up?"

"Jus follow me." The lumberjack grinned his toothy smile and gestured. "I weel show you."

He led Levi across the camp grounds to a corral built of newly hewn saplings. A large horse trough stood at the gate and the animals thrust their heads into it snorting and blowing as they quenched their thirst. "Thank you kindly," Levi said, proffering his hand. "The name's Levi Wakeford. Devereau's hired me and my team for the winter."

The little man pumped Levi's hand in a strong clasp matching his own.

"Pierre LaBeau welcomes you to camp." he said heartily.

Michigan winters come fast and cold. By the middle of December there was a foot of snow on the ground and the temperature dipped well below freezing at night. The packed snow made the logs easier to pull out of the forest and work went briskly.

It was not going to be easy to see Jenny before Christmas but Levi had a plan. They would need one more load of supplies before the camp was snowed in for the winter. He struck a bargain with Claude Devereau to go into Wolverine with his team and bring back a wagon load.

He hitched up Star and Robin long before daybreak and was on his way accompanied by Pierre. Levi liked this French Canadian. It was true that Pierre had a way of disappearing when there was work to be done, but he always had a story to tell and he was good company on a long ride.

It was late afternoon before Levi had all the sacks of flour, sugar, and other supplies loaded. The LaBlanc farm was five miles out of the way but Levi was determined to see Jenny one more time before the long winter set in. They started down the Afton road. Hidden inside Levi's coat was a small parcel, his mother's gold locket carefully wrapped in a piece of cotton. It was the only thing from his past he had to share with Jenny and nothing was going to stop him from delivering it on this cold December night.

They pulled into the LaBlanc farm just before dark. George and Frank stood on the porch to greet them. They crossed the barn yard as the wagon came to a stop. Levi tethered the horses. His eyes hidden by the brim of his hat, searched the house for signs of Jenny.

The LaBlancs recognized Pierre as an old friend and greeted him heartily in French, their welcome toward Levi more cautious.

"What brings you out this way?" George asked sizing up the load of supplies. "Shouldn't you be headed toward camp?"

The front door flew open before Levi could answer and Jenny came running down the steps. She stopped, just short of flying into his arms. She held her shawl tightly around her, a smile lighting up her face.

"Told you I'd be back before Christmas," Levi spoke softly for her ears only. Trying to control the urge to pull her to him, he took her small hands in his. He gazed down at her wind teased hair and glowing cheeks. "Don' you LaBlancs have a drink for a thirsty man?" Pierre clapped the two men on the shoulders urging them towards the house.

"Always, for a friend," George agreed, "How about you Levi?"

"I have to see to the horses," Levi mumbled.

"Don't be staying out in the cold, Jenny," he called as the men propelled him toward the house.

"I'll be there in a minute, Pa."

As soon as the door closed Levi pulled her to him and they embraced hungrily. Separation had been hard and they clung to each other. Levi gently pulled away reaching into his coat. "I've brought you present," he said, thrusting the small package into her hands.

"It's lovely," Jenny's voice quivered with emotion as she picked up the dainty gold chain. "Help me put it on." She lifted her thick tresses from her neck and Levi's big hands fumbled with the clasp. When he at last fastened it, he sealed it with a kiss on the fragrant nape of her neck and felt a shiver go through her small body as her arms flew around his neck. Time stood still for them but all to soon the moon rose in the black sky and Levi knew he had to go.

Jenny ran to the house to fetch a scarf she had knitted for him. "Levi says he's leaving," She called to Pierre as she ran past.

The men clapped each other on the back and said their farewells. Stepping out on the porch they caught Levi and Jenny in one last embrace. George and Frank scowled but Pierre laughed. The lovers didn't care. It would be the last they would see of each other for many months.

Jenny stood by the door watching until Levi and Pierre were out of sight. When she turned, her cheeks were still flushed from the memory of Levi's kisses but she held her head high and went in to face her family.

The full moon rose and Levi was thankful for the light. The wagon rattled along the deeply rutted road.

"Tha's some fine woman you got there." Pierre teased.

Levi nodded in agreement. The scarf Jenny had given him warmed his neck and it was hard to keep his mind on the heavily laden wagon. They moved slowly as the horses strained to pull through patches where snow had drifted across the road. Levi pulled the team to a halt when they reached the Pigeon river bridge. The water rushed below them in the darkness. The animals stomped their hoofs nervously on the wooden planks.

"They wan' get home. They're cold and tired like me."

"That's not it," Levi said getting down to check the reins. "They're used to much worse than this."

"Come my fran, have something for the cold." Pierre urged pulling a small flask from his coat, "Let's be on our way. Levi ignored him and with a final inspection of the horses, they started out again. When they reached the crest of a small hill and the moon lit up the meadow below.

"Let's have some fun with those cows," Pierre said laughing and pointed at the black shapes of animals in the field to the right. Before Levi could stop him he had pulled his shotgun from under the seat and fired in the air.

"You damn fool!" Levi cried, trying frantically to calm the horses. They weren't the only animals aroused.

Out in the field, one of the dark shadows slowly rose on its hind feet to a height of ten feet.

"Mon Dieu! eets Black bear!" Pierre cried out in alarm.

The horses, crazed with fear, plunged wildly down the road. Only the weight of the loaded wagon prevented them from running any faster. As it was, the wagon careened dangerously. Levi pulled frantically on the reins and Pierre clung to the seat.

Behind them a huge black form was closing in. Pierre turned and managed to fire his gun. A piercing roar of agony filled the night but as the first bear rolled away another approached running along the side. Pierre tried vainly to reload as the wagon bumped wildly.

Levi, still trying to control the team, looked down and saw the bear gaining on them. Its white fangs gleamed as it lunged toward Robin. Grabbing the reins with one hand he swung the whip and caught the animal full across the eyes. With a roar, it rolled away from the horses down the embankment. Pierre had his gun loaded now and fired twice. The animal lay where it had fallen.

The immediate danger was over, however, the team in full panic, raced madly down a small incline. Levi pulled the reins with all his strength, but there was no stopping the frightened horses. The wagon tilted wildly back and forth. Just before they reached the bottom of the hill the wheels caught in a rut and the wagon flew in the air landing on its side. Levi and Pierre were thrown into the ditch.

Luckily, the deep snow broke their fall. Levi scrambled to his feet and ran after the horses. The weight of the wagon had brought them to a halt but they rared, frantic with fear as he ran toward them.

"Easy now, Star," Levi spoke gently as he approached them, "That's it. Steady Robin. The horses slowly reacted to his voice and stood snorting, sweat glistening their hides. Upon closer inspection he found Robin's harness was broken and dangling. His back leg oozed blood from a gash where the whiffle-tree had struck him.

Levi gently removed the harnesses and led the animals to a small tree by the side of the road. He tied them and turned to inspect the wagon. Bags of flour were torn open, their contents strewn down the road. Kerosene dripped from a dented container. Luckily, the wagon wheels seemed to be intact. "Did you see how I shot that one?" Pierre came limping into view. "You're wan' lucky man to have Pierre along."

When Levi slowly turned to face him, Pierre's smile faded. The moon shown brightly on his face. From under the brim of his hat his eyes had become small pinpoints of light and his look of pure hatred sent Pierre backing away.

"You fool!" Levi's voice was a harsh whisper, "Look what you've done!" He strode toward the smaller man with purposeful steps.

Pierre ran around the side of the wagon. His eyes were wide with fear as he looked at the face of man ready to kill.

"What's the matter with you?" Pierre's voice rose shrilly. "I meant no harm."

"No harm?" Levi's cold voice hung in the silent night. "You almost got us killed. Robin's leg's cut. Half the supplies are ruined!" Levi moved to the end of the wagon and lunged but Pierre was quick and darted away from his grasp.

"Are you crazy?" The small man pleaded, "I am your fran. Why you want to hurt me?"

With a cry of fury, Levi threw himself at Pierre who tried vainly to defend himself. The two men rolled in the snow, fists flying. Strong fingers wrapped around the smaller man's throat as Levi pounded the frenchman's head to the ground. The sound of horses hooves brought Levi's fury to a halt. His eyes seemed to re-focus as he looked up to see Robin, his lines loosened, had broken away. Levi dropped Pierre's limp body and ran to retrieve his horse.

Levi untied Star and jumped astride his broad back. Robin's bleeding leg prevented him from getting too far and Levi soon overtook him. He grasped the dangling reins and slowly let the horse back to the overturned wagon where Pierre sat, clutching his throat, his eyes wide with fear.

"Get up and help me right the wagon," Levi's voice was normal now and Pierre with a sigh of relief got down to help him.

First they unloaded the supplies. With much shoving and pushing and the help of the team they were finally able to pull the wagon upright. It took them some time to sort the damaged supplies trying to salvage what they could. While Pierre finished tying them down, Levi re-worked the harness with an extra leather strap he carried under the seat. The jagged wound on Robin's leg was still bleeding and Levi tried to stench the flow by tying his kerchief tightly around it.

At last, he hitched up the horses and climbed into the driver's seat.

Pierre was pulling himself up next to him when he felt Levi's hand giving him a push. He landed in the snow. "The horse is hurt and can't pull the weight. You'll have to walk." Levi's said, pulling away.

"Sacre Blue!" Pierre shouted in dismay. "I save you're miserable life, help you weeth the wagon, and thees is the thanks I get?"

The wagon slowly rolled away leaving the angry Pierre sputtering behind.

"Jus wait til we get back to camp. Everyone will know what you have done. I weel tell Devereau what a crazy man you are and he'll send ayou away.!"

Pierre shook his fist at the wagon disappearing ahead of him and trudged along muttering as the snow flakes began to fall.

CHAPTER THREE

Winter of 1888

The winter snows bore down on the LaBlanc farm with a fury. Jenny rubbed a small patch of frost from the window. In the fading afternoon light she could make out Frank bending to the wind in the swirling snow as he attemped to clear the road into the farm with a roughly hewn plow made of two logs. She heard the dull thuds of her father's spade as he worked to break the layer of ice on the watering trough outside the barn.

"What is this word?" Marie asked, pointing to her primer. It had been impossible for the girls to attend school for several weeks. Jenny was helping them with their studies.

Jenny glanced down at the book. "Affection."

"Is that what you have for Levi?" Marie and Dehlia burst into giggles.

"If you want my help you'd better behave yourselves." Jenny replied briskly, trying to show her advantage of six years over her sister. "I think it's time for you to practice your sums." The girls sobered and took out their slates. Jenny assigned problems from the book mechanically. Her thoughts were with Levi. What was he doing? Was he out in the cold? Was he thinking of her? She remembered their last kiss and a warm glow filled her body. Turning her flushed face away from her sisters, she strained to look out the window again.

A lone horse and rider were coming down the road and Frank waved in recognition. Jenny watched the rider dismount and greet Frank and her father. When she saw how short he was, she knew it wasn't Levi and turned away with disappointment from the window.

When the door banged open with a blast of cold air she recognized the ruddy face of Herman Trubec. He and Frank had worked together at the sawmill in Cheboygan and he had been to the house several times. Jenny had not liked the way his beady eyes had followed her and had made it a point to stay busy in another part of the house when he was there but she was curious about his visit.

"Come in from the cold, Herman." Mrs. LaBlanc greeted him warmly. "What brings you out this way?". A visitor was an event and they were all eager to hear any news.

"I was on my way to Wolverine for Claude Devereau." Herman said, holding his hands out to the cook stove in the corner. "The wind started to pick up and with the snow drifting I figured I'd better look for a place to stop until it passed over."

"Take off your coat and set a spell," Mrs. LaBlanc urged, "Jenny, get Herman a cup of coffee."

Reluctantly, she poured a mug from the pot on the stove. As she neared the table the wet, rancid smell of the man almost overcame her and it was all she could do to set down the coffee and turn away.

His eyes followed her and nothing escaped his gaze. Her tiny waist encircled by a crisp white apron and her full skirts that swished as she crossed the kitchen. He smiled when a tiny auburn ringlet escaped from her snood and she nervously pushed it back.

"You're working for Devereau?" Jenny, Overcoming her repugnance of the man, had to ask. "Have seen Levi Wakeford?"

"What's a girl like you interested in the likes of him for?" Herman frowned

"She's sweet on him," Frank laughed as he sat down at the table with his friend.

"What do you mean, 'The likes of him', Herman?" Jenny demanded hotly.

"Don't get all riled up now. It's just that he's got a reputation for a bad temper and everyone stays clear of him. You'd do well to do the same."

"You don't know what you're talking about! Levi is twice the gentleman you are, Herman Trubec and he wouldn't hurt a fly.". Jenny turned her back on the smiling men and flounced across the kitchen. She took a large piece of dough from a pan on the stove where it had been rising and began to knead and pound it with vengeance. She ignored the men as they passed her going in to the parlor.

She helped her mother in silence, slicing carrots and rutabagas into the venison stew. Marie and Dehlia set the table with heavy blue china plates.

They placed steaming bowls and platters of hot biscuits on the table and called the men to supper.

George, Frank and Herman made short work of the meal. Levi's name was not mentioned. Mrs. LaBlanc beamed when Herman asked for a third helping of pumpkin pie. Jenny turned away in disgust.

After the last dish was put away and the kitchen swept, Jenny stubbornly refused to sit in the parlor to hear anymore of what Herman had to say. She climbed to the loft over the kitchen she shared with her sisters. The two younger girls were already settled down into their warm quilts. Jenny sat on the edge of her tick mattress plaiting her hair. Her thoughts as usual, were of Levi. "What right did Herman have to talk about him that way?" The wind howled angrily around corners of the house. She slid between the feather quilts with a shiver. As she had guessed, Mrs. LaBlanc had insisted Herman spend the night on the horsehair sofa. The men's voices drifted up from the kitchen where they were sharing the applejack jug. Jenny didn't pay any attention until she heard Levi's name mentioned.

"Damn near killed Pierre. Tipped over a load of supplies and tried to say it was Pierre's doin." Herman's voice droned on. "Never saw Devereau so mad! If he didn't have that strong team of Bays, Wakeford would have got his walkin' papers." *There must be some* mistake. Levi was the gentlest man she had ever known. He wouldn't hurt his friend Pierre. Not like her father and brother who got loud, nearly coming to blows if Mamma didn't stop them. Especially when they had been at the jug. But, Levi never even took a drink!

Nagging thoughts came to torment her, however. What did she really know about this man she had pledged her love to? She remembered the day they'd met. It was a blazing hot, Fourth of July. The LaBlancs had all piled into the wagon to drive to Wolverine for the annual celebration. They could hear music coming from the town square a mile before they got there.

Jenny helped carry baskets to tables set up on planks across sawhorses, setting out plates of fried chicken and biscuits covered with towels to protect them from the ever present flies.

Mrs.LaBlanc soon found a group of ladies to gossip with. Jenny went to join the Mueller sisters under a large oak. "Why are you watching some silly horse race?" she asked. "Let's go get some lemonade."

"Oh Jenny, we're not looking at the horses," Trudy whispered. "Look at that handsome stranger with his team of Bays. My Pa says he stands to chance of beating Cromwell's Grays."

Jenny turned in the direction her friend had pointed. A tall man with a formidable black mustache, moved with easy grace as he ran his big hands expertly over the horses and their harnesses.

"Don't see what's so handsome about him," Jenny scoffed. "His face is too thin and I don't much like mustaches." She had begun to turn away when the stranger removed his hat, running his hand through a thick shock of black hair. He turned and his grey blue eyes, under heavy brows, locked with hers. He tipped his hat and returned to the horses. Jenny found her heart racing. She leaned against the oak, her knees suddenly weak.

"Didn't we tell you?" Erma giggled. "I wonder who he is?" Jenny wasn't listening. She had fallen in love the very moment she had gazed into those intent eyes.

The race was the most popular event of the day. For the last three years John Cromwell's team of Greys had won easily. However, there was always a great deal of excitement and bets made between neighbors hoping to see Cromwell's team get beaten This year there were four teams involved. They ran two at a time and the winners of the first two races ran against each other for the final outcome. A course was set up in the field behind the livery stable. It ran a hundred yards to the edge of the trees, around two barrels, up a small hill and ended just behind Homer Clews' blacksmith stall.

The men hung over the fence watching excitedly at Peter Olmstead lined up his team against the stranger's matched horses. George and Frank LaBlanc cheered as the Bays finished a full twenty yards ahead of Olmstead.

Cromwells's team won easily over Landry's chestnuts. There was much talk and furious betting while the two winning teams got in place. George had long wanted to see Cromwell's team get beaten. He had lost to him two years ago and was tired of Cromwell's bragging. He and George studied the stranger's team. They were magnificent animals. Strong muscles rippled beneath their shining flanks. Hoping at last Cromwell had met his match, he placed several bets.

The shotgun went off and the two teams raced ahead, they're drivers urging them on. At the turn, Cromwell's team had a slight lead and George's hopes began to fade. As they came over the hill, however, the team of Bays had caught up and were slowly passing Cromwell's Greys. He whipped his horses furiously but could not catch the strangers team. George gleefully collected from several farmers and he and Frank went to look for the stranger that had finally beaten Cromwell. They found him leading his horses to the water trough. "That's some team you got there!" he called to the stranger. "Come have a drink with us."

"Thank you kindly, but I have to see to my horses," he said. Much to the dismay of all, the stranger walked calmly away leading his horses to the corral.

Jenny stood by the fence in the shadows of the Oak watching, noting the way his muscled shoulders moved as he poured cooling buckets of water over the animals.

"Would you like to feed them?" he asked. Without turning to look, he knew she was there.

"If they don't bite," she replied.

"No call to worry about that," He said, slowly walking the huge animals toward her. "They purely love carrots." He handed her a bunch from a gunny sack he was carrying. She held them out tentatively and the big velvet noses nibbled daintily from her fingers.

"They're really quite gentle," she turned in surprise to see his steady gaze on her, "Mr.—What is your name?"

"Levi, ma'am. Levi Wakeford." he said, a slow smile crossed his serious features. "And you'd be?"

"Jenny LaBlanc." she remembered replying as she gazed into blue eyes that took her breath away and come spring, she intended to marry Levi, the man she loved.

CHAPTER FOUR

Spring of 1888

It was the last week in March before Levi could leave the Devereau camp. It had been a hard winter. After the episode with the wagon Claude had reluctantly kept him on, with the understanding that he stay out of the bunkhouse. He'd been given a worn cot in the cookhouse. This didn't bother Levi. The cook, Marcell Vergo, spoke little English and ignored him. It was very lonely but the heat from the giant cookstove kept the room warm and after a fourteen hour day of driving his team through the snow covered trails he was to tired to do more than read a few passages from his bible before sleep overtook him.

Now all that was behind him. He had settled up with Devereau that morning and tucked his earnings of One hundred and fifty dollars securely away in a leather pouch hung on a thong inside his shirt.

The roads were muddy with the spring thaw and the half melted ruts made the going slow. He stopped in Wolverine and arranged to leave Robin with Homer Clews. The horse's leg had healed but he would always have a slight limp. As Levi left the blacksmith shop two boys rounded the corner in a rush, nearly knocking him down.

Levi grasped each of the boys by the collar. "Hold on there," he said sternly, "Just where do you two scamps think you're going in such a hurry?"

"Please, mister," the older freckled faced boy pleaded, "My brother needs to use the privy." Levi looked down the street in the direction the boy was pointing. There, right in front of Cromwell's store on main street stood a bright red outhouse. By it's size he figured it must be a six holer. Levi shook his head. Wolverine was really becoming quite a town. He turned the boys loose, admonishing them to watch where they were going in the future. He couldn't abide children that didn't mind their manners. If he ever had any younguns' they'd be taught right!

After purchasing a loaf of bread and a wedge of hard cheese, Levi set off astride Star for Cheboygan. It took him the better part of the day to get there. Coming into the town just before dusk he was impressed by the busy streets. Horse and carriages moved briskly along. Lanterns were being lit and yellow light shown from the store windows. He hadn't seen that many people in one place since he had left Albany. A frown flickered across his face. He didn't want to think of the past or its problems.

Searching the many places of business, he found what he was looking for. The sign read, "LIVERY STABLE-ROOMS" He quickly made arrangements for the horse to be fed and climbed the outside stairs to a room above the stable. He lit the kerosene lamp given him by the owner and looked around the room. He saw an iron bed with a stained tick mattress in one corner. A small dresser with a pitcher and basin made up the rest of the sparse furnishings. It would do. He washed his face and hands in the icy water, smoothed back his hair, and left in search of food.

Across the street, a Hotel caught his eye and he entered the huge lobby with pillars rising to a thirty-foot ceiling. Heavy chairs upholstered in red velvet matched the drapes that hung from tall windows. A shiny mahogany check-in desk stood at the corner next to the stair case. Levi turned to leave. To expensive for his pocket. However, smells of food coming from the dining room knotted his stomach and he relented.

"We're crowded tonight," the rosy cheeked matron told him. "You'll have to share a table." She lead the way to the back of the dining room. A man sitting by himself, looked up and frowned slightly noting Levi's rough appearance.

"If you'd rather eat alone, sir—" Levi said, hesitated.

"No, no, sit down." the man motioned to an empty leather backed chair. "Thought you were one of those damned Franchies that can't speak English." The man's stained vest pulled at the buttons over his ample stomach. "The chicken and dumplin's are pretty fair tonight." He said, motioning to his plate swimming in yellow gravy. The man sopped up the remains with a large biscuit licking his lips.

"I believe I'll try what the gentleman is having," Levi said to the plump waitress. He coughed to cover up the loud churning of his empty stomach. His mouth watered in anticipation . It had been many months since he'd tasted anything but salt pork and Marcel's johnny cake.

"Homer Rutledge's the name," The man wiped his gravy fingers on the edge of the tablecloth and extended his pudgy hand. "I own the Cheboygan Gazette."

Levi introduced himself and was soon telling the man he was in town to purchase a land grant.

"Levi Wakeford? Seems like I've heard that name before." Rutledge said peering closely at him. When Levi didn't volunteer any further information, the man shrugged and attacked a huge slice of apple pie.

"So you're going for a parcel of land?" the man said pushing his empty dish aside. He sat back to watch as Levi began to devour the plate of golden chicken and feathery dumplings the waitress set before him.

"One thing you ought to make sure of, is that there's water close by." Rutledge leaned back and lit up a cigar, blowing smoke up into the beamed ceiling. "Heard tell there's some sections along the Pigeon River still available."

"Thanks for the advice," Levi said, "I'll be sure and look into that." "Are you planning to put up a cabin?" The man asked.

"Yes sir," Levi told him mopping up the last crumbs from his plate, "As soon as I can get one built I plan to marry."

"Congratulations! Never took the step myself and sometimes regret it." The man looked sad for a moment but then went on.

"Just remember, don't build to close to the river. Come spring, you could be flooded out." Giving this advice, the man sat back belching contentedly.

"Much obliged," Levi said, enjoying the conversation with this learned man, "I'll remember your what you said."

"How about splitting a bottle of wine in honor of your upcoming marriage?" Rutledge suggested.

"Sorry, I don't partake of the grape," Levi said, "But I'll gladly buy you a drink, sir."

It was a rare thing to find a man who did not drink but had no objection to another doing so. Rutledge accepted his offer and Levi magnanimously paid the twenty-five cents for the dark whiskey the waitress brought.

"If I can be of any help to you, young man, look me up at the Gazette," Rutledge said as they shook hands and parted.

Many years later Levi would remember Rutledge's advice about the river and question his wisdom but at the time it made good sense. The next morning Levi rose with the first light and was waiting at the Land Office when it opened. A small man with a fringe of white hair and spectacles perched on the end of his nose motioned Levi to a large map hanging on the wall.

"The plots that don't have X's on 'em are the ones that are still left," the man told him.

Levi inspected the map carefully. He traced the Pigeon river with his finger. It ran parallel to the larger Sturgeon river. He was familiar with the area. There was a section just northeast of Wolverine. The Pigeon river ran through the western portion. Levi made up his mind. This 80 acres of land was the parcel he wanted.

"The land sells for $1.25 an acre." The clerk told him, his quill pen poised above the ledger. "You have two years to clear the land and farm it. If you fail to do so, the land will revert back to the government."

Levi nodded his agreement and counted out five twenty-dollar bills. The man carefully wrote out a description of the property, signed his name and stamped it with an official seal.

"Good luck, young man." The clerk smiled at him. "May you and your land prosper."

Levi shook the man's hand. "Thank you, sir." he said, folding the deed carefully and placing it in his inner coat pocket. The land was his! He couldn't wait to get back and tell Jenny.

CHAPTER FIVE

Summer 1888

 Levi went straight to the LaBlancs and asked for Jenny's hand. George wasn't too happy about this stranger taking his daughter away but he had to admit he was a hard worker and also a man of property. He also noted the way the two looked at each other and knew there would be little he could do to keep them apart.
 Levi and Jenny chose a piece of land at the top of a grassy hill to build their cabin. You could see the twisting river shining throughout the trees just a mile away.
 Levi set up a small camp and worked from dawn until darkness clearing the land and cutting down the tall pine trees for the logs he would need for the walls.
 He made one trip into town for supplies. He stopped at the mill to purchase two-by-fours and shingles for the roof. Next he went to Cromwell's hardware to buy nails, a hammer, two sturdy saws and a length of rope. He carefully counted out his money. He would need a cookstove and perhaps a pane of glass for a window but that could wait. He had to save enough to purchase seed to plant once he cleared more land.
 Levi had been working on his land for several weeks and the progress was slow. One morning He was pounding nails into the frame of the cabin when he looked up in surprise to see the LaBlancs pulling into the clearing with a full wagon. George and Frank climbed down and began unloading saw horses and a variety of tools.
 Mrs. LaBlanc handed down baskets of food to the girls. Levi

stood dumbfounded. In his surprise and confusion he became aware of Jenny running to him. He dropped his hammer and waited. She threw herself into his arms happily, straining on tiptoe for a kiss. He felt his knees threaten to buckle with the sweet fragrance of her in his arms.

"Pa and Frank are going to help you build our cabin," she cried breathlessly "Then Ma and I are going to fix you a real meal." She felt Levi stiffen.

"That's mighty kindly of you folks but I'm doing just fine by myself." Levi pointed to the cabin. "You can see I've got the floor and the framework almost done."

"Levi, don't be so stubborn," Jenny stamped her small foot. "This is my family and they will soon be yours. They've come to help you build *our* cabin." Looking down at Jenny's pleading face and at the two LaBlanc men waiting. "Guess I could use some help." he admitted.

By the time the sun was directly above, the cabin was taking shape. Marie and Dehlia gleefully picked wild flowers on their way from carrying pails of water from the river. Mrs. LaBlanc spread a sheet over a wooden plank set across two saw horses and she and Jenny placed loaves of fresh bread and apple butter on it. There were thick slabs of Salt Pork and baked beans along with hard boiled eggs. The men were more than ready to make short work of the feast when they were called to lunch.

When the last crumbs were gone the LaBlancs and Levi returned to the task of finishing the cabin. Jenny helped her mother pack up the dishes with one eye on how her house was coming along.

Sometime later Mrs. LaBlanc looked up and was horrified to see her eldest daughter halfway up a ladder lifting a plank of wood up to Levi. "Jenny! Come away from there," she admonished, "That work is for the men."

Levi smiled to himself as he heard her answer, "But Mamman, this is going to be my house and I want to help." Mrs. LaBlanc insisted and reluctantly, Jenny joined her mother and sisters in the shade. Before long, however, she was soon was running back to carry nails or other needed supplies. The cabin began to take shape and as Levi hammered away on the roof he knew he was truly grateful for the unexpected help from the LaBlancs. He had hoped Jenny's father would drop his objections when he learned of Levi's property but although George agreed to their marriage he had said very little and still seldom spoke. Now it seemed he had finally given his approval and his and Frank's help confirmed it.

By the end of the day the log walls were up and the roof was in place. They had done in one day what would have taken Levi weeks to do by himself.

Levi was shaking hands and thanking the LaBlancs for their help when Jenny stepped to his side sliding her small arm around his waist. "Think you can finish up the rest in two weeks?" she asked, gazing up at him with her brown eyes sparkling.

"There's the door to hang and a few other things to do," Levi said slowly, "Guess I could have it done. Why do you ask?"

"Because, Father LaSalle is coming in two weeks and we could be married while he is here."

Levi looked into her eager face and felt his longing for her rush through his body. "The cabin will be ready." he said bruskly, trying to control his voice and wild beating of his heart. On a bright spring morning in May 1888 Levi standing stiffly in his high collar, his unruly hair plastered flat, took the lovely Jenny LaBlanc to be his wife. The scent of apple blossoms drifted through the open windows of the church. Father LaSalle smiled the young couple before him. Jenny wore a dress of white dimity with blue satin ribbons. Her auburn curls hung from the white lace bonnet she wore. She shyly extended her tiny hand for the thin gold band that Levi nervously placed upon her finger. The priest pronounced them man and wife and they sealed their vows with a kiss that raised many an eyebrow in the small church.

The couple turned and walked out of the church to their family and friends. Mrs. LaBlanc cried as she embraced her daughter.

"Be a good wife to Levi and make your mamman proud," she said wiping her eyes.

George kissed his daughter awkwardly and shook Levi's hand. He was family now.

Friends and relatives from Wolverine and Afton congratulated and teased the young couple while they pretended to eat a large meal prepared in the church yard. Finally Jenny and Levi escaped to their waiting wagon pulled by Star and Robin. Jenny's sisters had decorated it with wildflowers.

Gifts from Jenny's parents included two pigs snorting nervously in the back of the wagon and a calf tethered behind. The newlyweds were on their way.

Levi pulled the wagon up before the waiting cabin. Jenny had not seen it since the day she and her family had come to help him. Levi opened the new oak door, picked up his bride and carried her into her new home. Rays of late afternoon sunshine filled the room from the roughly hewn window. A shiny new cookstove stood against the back wall with a supply of kindling.

Above, a shelf with sacks of flour and other supplies. A dry sink stood next to it with a bucket of water from the river. A rough plank table and benches sat under the window. To the left Levi had made a bed frame from fresh saplings. He looked anxiously to see if Jenny was pleased with his work. It was a far cry from the LaBlanc's comfortable farm but it was her new home and she loved it.

"You've worked so hard," she said smiling up at him, "It's just beautiful."

Levi helped Jenny carry in her belongings including a small trunk filled with linens and dishes. He left her putting things away while he saw to the animals.

When he entered the cabin she had changed from her wedding dress into a white cotton nightdress and was a arranging a feather mattress on the bed. Levi stopped short. His blood raced at the sight of her.

She turned to him, smiling. He carefully set down the lantern he was carrying. In three long steps he crossed the room and swept her up in his arms.

"I aim to get a pane of glass for a proper window before it gets cold," he said, his rough cheek resting on the top of her soft hair.

"I don't mind the fresh air," Jenny said, looking up into his face. Her finger traced the mustache she had grown to love.

"I'll build you cupboards and fix the cabin up fine for you," he said, kissing her fingers, her palms, her neck.

"I know you will," she said, trembling with excitement as his big hands fumbled with the buttons of her nightgown.

"We'll have to carry water from the river until I can dig a well." His voice was husky as his hands slowly raised her gown.

"I won't mind," she breathed in his ear.

Levi lifted her gently onto the soft feather mattress. The tall pines whispered and the sweet smell of cedars drifted in through the cabin window as they consummated their marriage.

Levi and Jenny's life together had begun.

CHAPTER SIX

February 1889

The winter snows all but buried the tiny cabin. Only a curl of smoke from the chimney showed any sign of life. It had been over two weeks since Levi had been able to take the animals to the river for water. Instead, he melted buckets of snow for the animals as well as themselves.

While the winds raged outside, the cabin was warm and cozy, however. Jenny, large with child, sat knitting. The first sharp pain took her by surprise. She had grown accustomed to the various discomforts as she grew larger but this was different. She waited quietly hoping desperately, she was wrong. The baby wasn't due for several weeks and she had hoped her mother would be able to come and help her when her time came. Another stab of pain made her gasp.

"Jen, what is it?" Levi looked up from the leather rein he was mending at his wife's white face. "Is it the baby?"

"I think so," she said. Fine beads of sweat formed on her upper lip. "Guess our son can't wait to get here."

"I should have took you to your ma's before the storm." Levi's voice shook. "Can't do it now." "It will be all right. I wanted our baby to be born here in our own home." Jenny smiled wanly at him as another pain shook her. "Don't you fret." she managed to gasp as the contraction eased, "I helped mamman when she had Dehlia. I know what to do."

Levi picked her up gently, kissed her forehead and lay her on the bed. "Tell me how I can help." he said brushing a damp curl back from her forehead.

"It probably won't be for some time yet," Jenny assured him. Why don't you go out and make sure we have plenty of wood for the stove." After much urging, Levi put on his heavy jacket and went outside.

Jenny removed her dress and replaced it with a flannel nightgown. She put a course blanket covered by a clean sheet on the bed and crawled under the quilts.

"I mustn't be afraid," she told herself. "Mamman told me what to do." She squeezed a small block of wood wrapped with clean rags tightly in her hand. When it became necessary she would bit down on it. Mamman said it would help.

A stronger pain racked her body and she clenched her small hands tightly until it subsided.

Willing her mind away from the present, she thought back to last summer. They had both worked hard. Clearing the land for planting had been an awesome task. Trees had to be cut down, underbrush burned off and stones carried. Jenny insisted on working side by side with her husband. By the end of June they had cleared four acres and Levi planted Oats, corn and one small section of potatoes.

Jenny found a sunny spot behind the house for her garden. Levi turned the rich dirt but the rest of the work was up to her. She planted rows of carrots, cabbage, onions, beans and rutabagas. When the hot summer sun beat down relentlessly she carried buckets of water from the river, a mile away, to the parched plants.

Levi tried to dig a well but after going down twenty feet he found nothing but hard stone. The river would have to supply their needs for now. His many other chores were more pressing at the moment. They did manage to set out a barrel to catch the rain and Jenny carried the rest of what they needed up the long hill from the river.

Levi, with an arm full of firewood, came through the door with a cold blast of swirling snow, momentarily chilling the room. He looked anxiously at Jenny's white face. She tried to smile.

"Can I get you something?" Levi stood watching his wife her pain reflected in eyes.

"If you could fix me a cup of tea ," she managed to say between clenched teeth, "With lot's of sugar."

"Sure thing. "Levi said, turning to the stove, eager to have something to do.

Jenny bit down the block of wood. My garden. I'll think about my garden, she told herself.

"It had been a constant battle with the rabbits and deer wanting to nibble the tender carrot tops and beans. Levi built some snares and they enjoyed rabbit stew on many occasions. Determined to keep the deer out of her garden, Jenny had tied string around the patch fastened to sticks waist high and tied white rags every few feet. It had been worth the trouble. The larder was full of vegetables she had grown. There would be enough to last well into the spring.

"Here, drink this," Levi held a steaming mug out to her. He steadied her trembling hand with his. She managed two sips before the next contraction racked her body.

"Strawberries. What I wouldn't give for one of those sweet strawberries that grow wild along the river bank." Jenny tried to smile at her husband. "Do you remember how many there were?"

"Seems I recall you eating too many and getting yourself sick," Levi reminded her, gently offering her another sip of tea.

"No, that was the blueberries that didn't set too well. They didn't bother you none, though, and you sure made short work of my pies." She tried to smile holding his hand next to her cheek but the next pain came and her fingers dug into his. Levi paced the floor from the bed to the door while Jenny tried not to cry outloud as the hours passed. He bathed her face, held her hand and paced some more as the pains became oftener and more severe. Sweat poured down her strained face.

It was in the early hours of morning when Levi rushed to her side as she let out an agonizing scream. Then he heard another smaller cry.

Levi and Jenny's first born son had entered the world.

Following Jenny's instructions, Levi tied the cord with string and cut it with his hunting knife. He wrapped the baby in a bleached flour sack and placed it in her arms. Levi blinked back tears as he looked into the white face of his wife smiling down at the tiny red one.

"What should we call him?" Jenny asked, cuddling the newborn close to her.

Levi thought for a moment and then he remembered his only close relative back in Albany. "I'd like to name him after my uncle Homer."

"Sounds fine to me," Jenny agreed and so Levi got down his bible and with a stubby pencil entered the name Homer Wakeford, their firstborn child.

CHAPTER SEVEN

August 1894

Jenny stood at the edge of the garden shading her eyes. Across the waving field of Oats she could see Levi and his team pulling the binder he'd borrowed from the LaBlancs. The cut grain lay in three foot long bundles. Homer, his straw hat shining in the afternoon sunlight, bounced on the back of one of the horses. A flicker of a frown crossed Jenny's brow. If the boy wasn't careful, he could fall off and he'd be under the horses or worse yet, the machinery, in seconds. She's asked Levi not to take him out in the fields but the boy followed his father everywhere.

She looked down at the little blond head of the babe in her arms. In another year Roy would probably be following his father around too. She shifted the boy to her hip. His chubby legs wrapped around her waist.

"Me too, mama," a tiny voice pleaded. Jenny smiled down at the red curls of her daughter pulling at her skirts.

"Mama can't carry both you and your brother," she cajoled, "You're a big girl now, Beatrice, you can help me pick beans."

"Don't wanna pick beans," the little girl stamped her bare foot in the dirt.

"Then go see if there are any berries left to pick. You know how you love them." Jenny sighed as the tiny figure in the white pinafore turned and ran down the path. She hated to admit it, but her three year old daughter was a handful. Beatrice was a stubborn, fretful child, unlike the quiet easy-going boys. Her howls and fits of temper were well known to her parents.

Jenny filled her apron with beans, planted a kiss on the child sleeping in her arms and turned toward the house. A new barn stood beside it now. Levi said they needed it for the livestock. The animals had survived other winters with a small lean-to and a haystack but she supposed he was right. At least there was a place for her chickens. Maybe next year, if the crops were good, Levi would build her a new house or at least add a room. With three children it was getting crowded and if she wasn't mistaken, another was on the way. She entered the cabin and lay the sleeping boy in his cradle. Emptying the beans from her apron on the table, she decided now would be a good time to go look for fresh eggs.

Jenny entered the dim barn and started searching in the usual spots, but only found two brown eggs. The hens were always finding new places to lay. Hearing clucking coming from the loft, she climbed the ladder. Sure enough, two of her Plymouth Rock hens were sitting on nests. Slipping her hand under the feathers she pulled out warm eggs, depositing them in her apron pockets.

Jenny stood for a minute at the open hay door. A fresh breeze cooled her sweating brow. She could see the river clearly from this point as it twisted it's way across the fields. She froze as she spotted a curly red head bobbing along the bank of the river. The child was much to close to the edge! "Dear God, don't let her fall in," she prayed.

"Beatrice, come back!" she screamed waving her arms frantically.

Jenny watched in horror as the tiny figure teetered for a moment and then tumbled down the riverbank. Turning to run from the loft she caught a glimpse of Levi in the field. He must have heard her cries. He pulled up the team and jumped down from the binder. She could see his tall frame running in the waist high, moving field of grain.

His long strides took him quickly to the riverbank. He parted the brush and in one swift move dove into the rushing water. He swam fiercely toward the white bundle floating towards him in the swift moving current. His fingers reached out and caught the red curls just as she floated past. He grasped the child tightly and swam for shore. Reaching the steep bank he pulled himself and the limp child up the incline. When he reached the top he stretched the still form of his daughter out on the grassy bank and began pressure on the small back. By the time Jenny burst through from the oat field sputtering wails could be heard. She dropped gratefully to her knees beside the crying child.

"Bad Papa," Beatrice choked between sobs, "He hurt my back."

"No, no child," Jenny said, cradling her in her arms. "Papa saved you from the river." The relieved parents stared speechless at each other over the head of scowling child. Without a word, Levi turned and went back to the fields. Jenny carried the soaking child back to the house. She was thankful her husband had not seen fit to punish Beatrice. He was very strict with the children and while she didn't always agree, she never interfered.

The next morning Jenny was busily scraping the remains of the breakfast pancakes into a bucket for the pig's swill when she was surprised to hear the ring of an axe. She'd thought Levi had gone out to the fields. Thinking no more about it, she skimmed the cream from the milk pail and set it aside. She was throwing sunflower seeds to the chickens when she saw Levi and Homer coming from the river. Her son was soaking wet but grinning from ear to ear. "Me and Pa have been swimming," he told her proudly.

"Fetch the other children and come down to the river," Levi told her.

"Have you lost your mind?" Jenny demanded looking at her husband and noting he was also wet. "After what happened yesterday, I'd think you wouldn't ever want the children near the river again."

"Just do as I say, Jen." Levi said sternly. She hesitated for a moment and then looking closely at her husband's set face, she went inside to scoop Roy up from the floor of the cabin where he was playing with wooden blocks. They found Beatrice coming down the outhouse path.

"Come along, girl, "Levi called, I've got something to show you."

When they approached the river, Jenny saw that Levi had cut down a tall sapling and that it reached across to the other bank of the river.

"You ready to show your Mama what you learned?" Levi asked Homer. The boy eagerly waded into the shallow water at the edge. Holding his nose, he jumped into the swift current. Jenny watched aghast, as the body of her son floated away. To her relief, he began to move his arms with the current and soon reached the log. He waved excitedly. "Did you see me swim, Ma?"

She turned to Levi, not sure if she should scold him or praise when she heard him saying, "Now Beatrice, I want you to swim like your brother." The girl began to howl and clung to her mother's skirts. In spite of her protests he picked up the kicking child and carried her into the river. The cold water momentarily quieted her screams.

"Just move your arms and kick your legs and the current will take you to the log," Levi told her, firmly taking her arms from his neck, he let her go.

Beatrice sputtered and shrieked as the current took her down the swirling river. Jenny cried out as her head went under. However, the wet curls soon surfaced and when she reached the log she clung to it howling with anger and fright.

Levi waded into the river and calmly let himself float down to the children. He scooped one up in each arm and brought them ashore.

"Levi! not again!" Jenny cried as he tossed the laughing Homer back into the water. Ignoring the cries of his wife and daughter, Levi calmly took Beatrice back into the water and let her go again. This was repeated several times until she began to kick her arms and legs.

At last, Levi let the children crawl up the grassy bank and rest.

"How could you frighten the children like that?" Jenny demanded, wiping their wet faces with her apron.

"They live next to a river," Levi said calmly, "If they don't learn to swim they could drown."

"Not Roy!" she said backing away, the baby clutched tightly in her arms.

Levi looked into the frightened face of his wife and said grudgingly, "We'll wait until he learns to walk."

Jenny still wasn't sure of Levi's wisdom as she took Beatrice by the hand and led her home. But, years later, on more than one occasion, she was grateful for his foresight in teaching the children to swim.

CHAPTER EIGHT

October 1898

"Pa! guess what me and Roy just saw?" Homer and his brother burst into the kitchen, their cheeks flushed with excitement.

"Is that any way to come into a house?" Jenny scolded, turning from the stove. "Where have you been anyway? You're Pa said grace without you."

"There's men across the river with horses and wagons!" Roy's high pitched voice rang out, "They're making a camp."

"What are you talking about, boy?" Levi demanded, looking up from his plate. "The land across the river belongs to us."

"It's true, Pa," Homer chimed in. "Me and Roy were watering the cows and we seen them down by the bridge."

"Do you think they could be loggers?" Jenny asked her husband as he rose from the table.

"We'll soon find out," Levi called back over his shoulder. Grabbing his hat, he headed for the door.

"Where do you think you're going, young lady?" Jenny caught Beatrice as she jumped from her chair and started to follow. "You stay here with me and Carl.

"But Mamma, I want to see, too," Beatrice argued, struggling to twist from her mother's grasp.

"No need for you to go." Jenny sat her down, depositing the rosy cheeked baby she had been carrying on her hip to her older daughter's lap. "You can feed Blanche."

"I never get to do anything." Beatrice pouted, making a face at the smiling infant who grabbed handfuls of her sister's red curls and pulled with glee.

Jenny put Levi's plate on the back of the stove to keep warm ignoring the squeals coming from her daughters. What if there was a logging camp going up nearby? They wouldn't dare cut trees on Wakeford land but they could set up camp down river. There would be noise and those wild lumberjacks would scare game for miles around. On the other hand, they were sure to keep the roads clear in the winter. A lumber camp could have it's merits.

Jenny took the crying Blanche from her sister and hushed her as the two younger children cleaned their plates. When they were done she set the dirty plates in the dry sink. Emptying the last of the water from a wooden bucket into the teakettle she placed on the stove, she sent Beatrice to fill it from the barrel outside.

Jenny sat down in the maple rocker, a gift from her father after the birth of Homer. It had been put to good use. As she rocked and nursed the baby her gaze traveled around the cabin. In the ten years they had been married Levi had added two rooms and built a porch off the kitchen but it was still crowded.

At the moment her hopes for a new house seemed dim. With a small sigh, she rocked and waited for Levi and the boys to return.

It was almost dark when they got back. Jenny searched the face of her husband. He didn't seem upset, but she couldn't always tell.

"They're from the Hillenbrand outfit." Levi said, dropping to his place at the table. "They're setting up camp about five miles the other side of the bridge."

"But why are they on our property?" Jenny asked setting Levi and the boy's warmed supper before them.

"You shoulda seen Pa," Homer piped up. "He told them they was trespassin' and to get off our land."

"That's enough," Levi cautioned, "Eat your vittles."

"Are you going to let them stay?" Jenny looked anxiously at her husband.

"It's just temporary until they can cut a road in to the site." Levi explained mopping up the last of the gravy on his plate with a thick biscuit.

"What if they cut down some of our trees?"

"Don't you fret, none." Levi smiled one of his rare smiles. "I plan to keep a close watch on 'em and if they cut any of our timber they'll pay for it. Besides, Hillenbrand is a big outfit and I just might be working for them this winter. The horses are getting along in years but they're still strong enough to haul logs.

"The fella I spoke to told me to come and see the foreman tomorrow. A man named Trubec."

"Herman Trubec?" Jenny turned to look at her husband.

"I do believe that's his name." Levi glanced up at his wife's worried face. "What do you know of him?"

"He used to work with Frank at the sawmill." Jenny hastened to explain. "Can't say I much liked him." She said turning back to the stove.

"Why was that?" Levi asked looking up at her puzzled by his wife's strong opinion.

"He was always braggin' and loud." she answered as she added kindling to the stove. There was no need to tell Levi how Herman had always stared at her with his half veiled leering ways. It had been years since she'd seen him and there was no need to upset Levi.

"If he hire's the team it'll sure help with the planting money," Levi avoided his wife's eyes. "Can you and the boys do the chores without me during the week?"

"Guess we could manage," Jenny said softly as she fought back tears that had sprung to her eyes. It would be the first time they'd been apart and she felt a sharp pang at the thought of their empty bed. She brushed the thoughts aside. The money Levi could earn would be a blessing. It had been a long hot summer and the crops had been poor. There was barely enough grain for the animals and the children all needed shoes.

That night Jenny lay in the curve of her husband's arm and prayed silently. If Herman Truabec would hire Levi and his team, she'd make herself be polite to him. The job meant so much to them all.

Things worked out better than Jenny had hoped. Not only did Levi get a job with his team but the camp cook said he would buy all the eggs, butter and milk they could spare.

Usually, McInnis the cook sent one of the boys he used as helpers to pick up supplies from Jenny but this week she decided to walk to the camp and settle accounts with him herself. She needed some spending money. Levi had promised to take her and the children with him the next time he went into town for supplies.

Jenny packed a basket with eggs and butter, putting it over one arm with baby Blanche bundled up in the other, she started out for the lumber camp.

It was a cold crisp day. She looked down at Carl who skipped happily along beside her. The older children were in school. He was such a joy! His black curls, so like his father's, hung down on his forehead from under his wool knit cap. He had Levi's blue eyes too, but unlike his sober father, they were always crinkled in a smile. They walked steadily down the wagon trail toward camp. Most of the trees were bare except for the tall pines. Carl picked up red oak leaves showing them proudly to his mother.

After a time the full basket became heavy forcing Jenny to set it down to rest. She shifted the sleeping child to the other arm and leaned her weight against a white birch to catch her breath. Carl ran on ahead. She looked up to see him coming back with a man in a dark red mackinaw jacket. She stiffened, when she saw the man was Herman Trubec.

"What brings you to camp, Jenny?" Herman asked, his eyes roving slowly over her still trim, figure.

"I've come to settle up the Mr. McInnis, the cook." she swallowed the words she wanted to say to that leering face.

"Here, let me carry that," he said, reaching for the basket. "What kind of man you got that lets his wife walk into a lumber camp alone?"

"My husband knows I can take care of myself," she said scooping the basket away, her chin raised defiantly.

"I tell you what, I wouldn't let no woman of mine walk into a camp of lumberjacks starved for the sight of a female." Herman said stepping closer, "Especially, a fine lookin' woman like you."

"That's really no concern of yours, Herman." Jenny walked briskly down the path, her cheeks flushed.

"I bet your husband don't know you're here." A sly smile played on his thick lips, "What's your secret worth?"

Jenny kept walking trying to ignore him.

"Maybe next time I'll come by your place to pick up the eggs and we can have a nice talk," Herman leered at her.

"You'd better not let Levi catch you near our place," Jenny said hotly, "He'd show you off in a hurry."

Just then the cookhouse door opened and Angus McInnis stepped out. "Miz Wakeford, here let me help you with that." He said, taking the heavy basket from her eyeing Trubec suspiciously.

"See you later, Miz Wakeford," Trubec smiled mockingly and turned away toward the camp.

"What brings you over her alone?" McInnis scolded, "I would have sent the boy tomorrow."

"I know, but I was wondering if I might set our account straight." Jenny stood inside the door, nervously holding the baby and Carl's hand in hers.

"Here, set yourself down," the cook said, hurriedly dusting off a barrel for her to sit on. "How about a nice cup of tea?" Jenny sat down, grateful to be in the warm kitchen filled with the smells of fresh baked bread.

The cook set a large plate of molasses cookies before them and Carl devoured several while Jenny sipped the hot tea laced with brown sugar. The baby slept in her arms.

McInnis pulled out a thick ledger from the cupboard and laid it on the table. Jenny and he compared notes and settled on an amount of ten dollars and fifteen cents owed her. He pulled out a drawstring purse from inside his shirt and carefully counted out the money. Jenny folded the bills and placed them in a pocket inside her short jacket. "Miz Wakeford," the little Scotsman looked embarrassed, "There's no need for you to walk over here again, carrying the wee bairn and all."

"I believe you're right, Mr. McInnis," Jenny admitted, "I didn't realize it was so far. I'll be going now and I won't come again."

"If you'd like, I can send the money with the lad when he comes to pick up supplies." The cook was much relieved to hear she wouldn't be coming back to camp. Any man could see she was a beautiful woman with that auburn hair of hers and those pink cheeks and he'd seen the way Trubec had looked at her.

Quickly he filled Carls pockets with cookies and ushered them out the door. The sooner they left the better.

"Mind your step now, Miz Wakeford," McInnis called to her from the doorway.

Jenny turned to study his ruddy face. What Was he warning her about?"

"The path has ruts. You wouldn't want to trip with the bairn." he said but his wise old eyes held another meaning.

Jenny pulled her shawl tightly around her and headed for home.

CHAPTER NINE

Jenny watched anxiously out the window for Levi's wagon. He had promised to take them into town on his way to get supplies for the camp. The sky was grey and overcast and the air had smelled like snow when Homer and Roy came in from milking. Maybe he wasn't coming.

At last, she heard the rattle of the wagon. The boys ran out to meet their father. Levi hopped down and left the boys to tend the horse while he strode to the house. He greeted Jenny with a tight embrace. They were not used to being apart. Feeling the swift beating of his heart against hers, Jenny knew he had missed her as much as she had him.

"Are you ready?" Levi asked gruffly, stepping back. Jenny nodded and picked up the baby.

"Let's get started then." Levi closed the door after them and gazed upwards. I don't like the looks of it out there. Could be a storm brewin'."

After checking to see if all the children had their coats buttoned and hats on, Jenny followed Levi to the wagon and climbed up onto the front seat. The boys hopped on the back of the wagon, their legs dangling over the edge. "I don't want to ride in the back. Its too cold." Beatrice stood with her small arms folded stubbornly looking up. "I want to be up front between you and Papa."

"Climb up here then, and be quick about it," Levi said impatiently, holding out his hand. Beatrice stuck her tongue out at her brothers as she snuggled between her parents.

"You won't have much time to do your shopping," Levi told his wife as they traveled down the rutted road. "I promised Trubec I'd be back before dark."

Jenny bristled at the name of Trubec. That man again! She had not told Levi about her encounter at the camp. She'd seen Levi's temper and thought it best not to mention the incident. Besides, she could handle the likes of Herman Trubec.

Levi pulled the team to a stop before Cromwell's General store and they all trooped inside. Levi had a long list from the camp to be filled and while they were getting his order Jenny checked bolts of fabrics.

Her fingers lingered over the dark blue cotton with tiny white flowers but she pushed it aside and selected four yards of heavy brown wool. If she cut it carefully she could make a shirt for Levi and there would be enough for the boys too. A bolt of green corduroy was next. Two yards would make Beatrice a warm coat.

The boys stood in awe before the sticks of cinnamon and peppermint candies in shiny glass jars but Beatrice eyes were on a china doll with a blue silk dress sitting up high on the shelf.

"It's good to see you Jenny," Mrs. Cromwell said measuring the material. Her round face kindly. "Saw your sister, Marie last week. She tells me she's planning to go to the big city of Detroit."

"Yes, she got a job down there," Jenny sighed, "Ma and Dehlia will truly miss her."

Jenny selected heavy thread, buttons and a small pack of needles. She carefully counted out her money. There was just enough left for one pair of boots. She called to Homer.

Mrs. Cromwell brought down a pair of sturdy black hightops from the shelf. Homer quickly undid his old boots and slipped his neatly darned stocking feet into the new pair. He proudly strode around the store showing them off. His old ones were carefully wrapped and given back to Jenny. They would go to the next child.

"I want new shoes too!" Beatrice cried, her voice rising to a high pitch. Farmers sitting near the back of the store looked up and shook their heads at the screaming child.

"You don't need new shoes," Jenny said firmly, taking her small hand and pulling her toward the front of the store.

"Do too!" Beatrice's shrill voice filled the store.

"You're goin' to make me wear Roy's old ones and they stink from cow dung." Jenny dragged the whining child after her. Her cheeks hot with embarrassment.

"I want the dolly," Beatrice said, planting her feet firmly as she pointed to the top shelf, howling to the top of her lungs.

If his daughter's outburst annoyed Levi, he showed no sign. He was anxiously looking out the window at the darkening sky.

"Here, give her one of these," Mrs. Cromwell said, offering a green striped peppermint stick. Beatrice howls subsided as she reached for the candy. She gave her brothers a self satisfied smirk as she licked the candy.

"Levi strode to the counter and laid down two copper pennies. "I'll take three more for the boys." he said scowling at his daughter. "Now, let's be on our way."

The Wakefords climbed aboard the loaded wagon. The boys sat between the sacks of onions and potatoes, sucking on their candy. Jenny pulled her shawl tightly around her and the sleeping baby as she felt the first snowflake on her nose.

It came down in fluffy white flakes at first. The boys shrieked with delight trying to stick handfuls down each other's backs.

As the snow got heavier they slid down between the sacks, just the brims of their hats sticking out. Jenny pulled her full skirt over Beatrice's knees and hugged her close.

The broad backs of the horses were all that could be seen ahead as the snow melted on their steaming flanks. Levi peered into the white swirling storm trying to see the road. They had been on their way for about an hour when the wagon lurched to the right. Beatrice roused from her sleep began to cry. "Hush child!" Jenny cautioned. Levi pulled the wagon to a stop and jumped down to see what was wrong.

"What is it?" Jenny called out.

Jenny heard the worry in Levi's voice. "The wagon's off the road and the back wheel is stuck." Through the white mist his form suddenly emerged beside her. "I think I can get the team back onto the road but you'll have to hold the reins."

"Beatrice, take the baby." Jenny thrust the sleeping infant into her arms and grabbed the reins.

The wagon lurched and groaned as Levi pushed and the horses snorted. Jenny said a silent prayer as she felt it finally move. She didn't want to think about how much trouble Levi would be in if he lost another wagon full of supplies.

"I'd best lead the team," Levi said disappearing ahead and urging the animals along.

Jenny clutched the reins. The only sound was the creaking of the loaded wagon and the jingle of the harnesses.

"Beatrice, get in the back with baby Blanche. Homer, make room for her and help her down." Jenny called over her shoulder.

"Why do I have to hold her?" Beatrice grumbled, sliding down between the sacks. "She'll probably wet and freeze me."

"Just do as your told!" Came her mother's voice. Beatrice, for once, knew when to stop. Actually it was much warmer nestled between the sacks and the baby's warm body felt good next to her.

Jenny's hands grew numb with the stiff reins wrapped around her fingers. The driving snow bit into her face but she put it out of her mind concentrating on the dim form of her husband.

A lone cry of a wolf howled somewhere to the left and Levi stepped back to pull his twelve gauge from under the seat.

"How much farther?" She shouted between chattering teeth.

"I figure we're almost to the bridge, should be home soon."

Jenny turned to check on the children. They were all snug between bags of supplies.

Only the tops of their hats and small spirals of their hot breath escaping could be seen through the snow covering. She turned back, hunching her shoulders and bowing her head to the driving snow.

She breathed a sigh of relief when she heard the horses hoofs clop on the wooden bridge knowing they were almost home. Soon they were pulling into their own barn. Jenny blew on her rigid fingers as she, at last, released the reins.

Levi and Homer stayed to feed and water the horses while Jenny herded the children back to the cabin.

"I'm cold," Beatrice wailed clinging to her mother.

Her mother ignored her. "Roy, bring in some wood. Carl, hold the baby while I get a fire started. Beatrice, let go of my skirts and light a lamp. By the time Levi and Homer returned from the barn a warm fire glowed in the cook stove and a teakettle simmered.

Jenny stared at her husband as he drank a cup of tea and headed for the door. "You're not going out in the storm!" she cried holding his arm.

"Promised Trubec I'd be back tonight."

Fighting back tears, she knew better than to argue.

CHAPTER TEN

"When's Papa coming," Beatrice rubbed the frost covered window trying to see out. "He promised he'd be home for Christmas."

"Is Santa Claus coming tonight?" Carl asked eagerly, sliding into his place at the table. Jenny forked a golden pancake onto his plate.

"What a baby," Beatrice scoffed, "There's no such thing as Santa Claus."

"There's too!" Carl insisted, "He brought me a slingshot and a top last year."

"You're so dumb." his sister scoffed. "Papa made those."

"That's enough, Beatrice," Her mother cautioned. "Santa only comes to good little children."

"That lets Stringbean Beatrice out," Homer hooted from his end of the table.

"Stop fighting and finish your breakfast. We've got a lot to do today. Homer, you take Roy into the woods behind the barn and find us a nice fir tree. Beatrice, you can help me bake gingerbread cookies and Carl can string popcorn." Jenny said laying the baby in its cradle.

"Should we chop the tree or wait for Pa," Homer asked.

"You'd better cut it down, "Jenny said turning from the table to hide a worried frown. She wasn't sure Levi would be able to get home before tomorrow. The lumber camp was not working on the holiday but they were expected to put in a full day's work on Christmas Eve. She was sure Trubec would keep them all working until dark.

Jenny went out to the barn and pulled two fat Plymouth rock hens from their roost and quickly rung their necks. She hated to part with laying hens but this Christmas was going to be meager and she wanted dinner to be special. Levi had a special fondness for roast chicken.

She carefully plucked the feathers and set them aside to be saved for mattress ticking. She thought of what still had to be done. She had finished the shirts for the boys and Levi. The rabbit muff for Beatrice still had to be lined. It would go with her new green corduroy coat. The rest of her gifts were knitted socks and mittens for all and a new bonnet for Baby Blanche. There wouldn't be any toys this year but they would enjoy the chicken dinner. It would have to do.

In the afternoon Homer and Roy returned, their cheeks rosy with the cold, pulling a large fir tree behind them. "Nail two boards crosswise to the bottom, like your father showed you," Jenny told them, "Come children, help me make room for the tree."

The fresh smell of the evergreen filled the room mingled with spicy ginger from the freshly baked cookies. Rows of cranberries and popcorn lay stretched across the worn oil cloth on the table, waiting to be hung. Roy and Homer pulled sturdy chairs across the wooden floor to stand on so they could reach the top branches. Beatrice stood back, arms folded, complaining they weren't doing it right.

Ignoring her, the boys carefully clamped tin candle holders onto the strongest branches. Short yellow wax candles were set firmly in place to be lighted later. Jenny set a pail of water in readiness next to the tree. If a draft caught one of the lit candles it could easily catch the tree on fire and it was best to be prepared. She stood back and nodded approvingly.

"Where's Papa?" Beatrice's voice whined. "He always holds me up so I can put the star on top."

"Let Homer hold you up." Her mother suggested.

"No, I want Papa." The little girl stamped her foot and clutched the tin star to her chest.

"Then you'll just have to wait until he gets home." Jenny told her, trying not to be too short with the child. It *was* Christmas Eve and she wished with all her heart that Levi would come home soon.

Jenny fed the hungry children fried potatoes with thick slices of salt pork, saving a plate on the back of the stove for Levi.

A welcome sound of harnesses jingling brought them all to their feet. "Go help your father with horses, Homer. Beatrice, put Papa's mug on the table."

Levi's big frame filled the door and over the shouts of the children Jenny gazed across the room at her husband. Their eyes locked in silent greeting and her heart beat with excitement as it always did. She looked closely as he swung Beatrice to the top of the tree where she placed the star triumphantly. Was there something in his yes. A secret? What was he up to?

"Here, McInnis sent this over," he said, thrusting a large gunny sack to his wife. There was a large fruit cake on top of tins of cookies. In the bottom her fingers closed with surprise around the firm shape of apples. What a treat the children would find in their stockings.

"McInnis is a kind man," Jenny said, remembering the day she had walked to the camp.

"He is, indeed." Levi agreed, surveying the room. "That's a fine tree," he said turning to Homer and Roy who blushed with their father's approval. He smiled one of his rare smiles and patted the younger children on their heads.

While Levi ate his supper the children sat expectantly on a thick braided rug in front of the tree inhaling it's piney scent. At last he pushed back his chair and said, "I believe it's time to light the tree.

Levi took a long tallow candle and lit it from the coals in the stove. One by one he ignited the candles on the tree. The children sat mesmerized as the small flames flickered and cast a golden glow over the thick branches. The shiny cranberries caught the light and shimmered.

When he had lit them all, Levi pulled his favorite sturdy chair close to the tree and began to read from his well worn bible. The children listened intently to his voice. "In those days a decree went out from Ceasar Augustus that all the world should be enrolled." An occasional snap of a pine cone popping open in the warmth of the cabin was the only other sound.

"But Mary kept all these things, pondering them in her heart." Levi concluded the story slowly closing his bible. Jenny's clear voice began to sing Silent Night and the others joined in. Beatrice sang as loud as she could, trying to drown out her brother's high sweet voices. Levi's deep baritone joined in, harmonizing with the rest. A warm glow surrounded the Wakeford family.

"Children, you best be getting into bed," Levi said as he rose to extinguish the candles. "Don't forget to give me your stockings to hang on the door for Santa Claus." Beatrice hurriedly thrust hers before Roy and Carl. "You too, Homer," Levi said, nailing the different size socks on the door. Homer gave his father a knowing look but handed over his stocking.

"Now you scalawags, let me see how fast you can all get to bed." He didn't have to tell them twice. They said they're prayers and were soon fast asleep.

"Levi Wakeford, just where do you think you're going?" Jenny asked later when she looked up and saw her husband reaching for his hat and jacket.

"Santa Claus," he said putting his finger to his lips, then he quietly slipped out the door.

Jenny waited, curious about what he was up to. When he hadn't returned for some time she pulled on her shawl and went out on the porch to look. To her amazement she saw fresh sleigh tracks in the new fallen snow leading up to the house. She peered into the darkness and saw Levi's tall form coming from the barn. He was brushing the snow behind him, obliterating all tracks of the sleigh.

Jenny's arms opened to embrace the gentle man who cared enough about his children's Christmas dreams to borrow a sleigh and pull it across the snow to leave evidence of Santa. They clung together, smiling as the moon peeked out from a cloud making the snow sparkle.

Inside, Levi emptied a sack he had brought from the barn. Jenny was astonished to see gifts for the children. There were small wooden horses carved in detail for Carl. A soft deerskin pouch with glass marbles for Roy. For Homer there was a shiny jackknife.

"Where did these all come from?" Jenny asked, tears glistening in her dark eyes.

"McInnis and some of the others at camp wanted the children to have them," Levi said gruffly.

Reaching deep into the bottom of the sack he brought out three more mysterious packages. "These are for my girls. Go ahead, open them." he urged.

Jenny carefully unwrapped the first long thin package and was stunned to see it revealed the china doll from Cromwells, Beatrice had wanted. The smaller package held a soft rubber ring for baby Blanche. Opening the last package Jenny could not control the tears rolling down her cheeks as felt the soft blue material with sprigs of flowers she had so admired.

"Don't fret, now," Levi pulled her to him, "I earned some extra money trapping Beaver." It was some time before she could tell him how much she loved him.

The next morning they awoke to hushed whispers. Roy had made an early trip to the outhouse and discovered the sleigh tracks. Soon all the children were staring out the window in disbelief. Levi put on a great show of rubbing his eyes and feigning surprise. "What's this?" he asked, pointing to the gifts.

"Did you hear Santa come in?" Levi asked Beatrice as she scooped up her doll dancing around the room with it.

"Of course I did." the little girl assured him. Jenny and Levi exchanged glances. "He had on a red suit and I asked him for my doll and he gave it to me."

"Is that so?" Levi shook his head at his small daughter, "Did you see him fill your stocking, too?"

The excitement of the presents they had all forgotten about them. Levi carefully took down the bulging stockings, handing one to each child. Their eyes widened at the hard candy canes and sugar drops. The boys quickly offered some of their sweets to their mother and father but Beatrice turned away clutching hers tightly. It was obvious she was not willing to share with anyone.

CHAPTER ELEVEN

March 1899

McInnis, looking out the window above his stove was surprised to see Trubec. What was he doing in camp? He was supposed to be out at the site overseeing the last of the cutting. Something about the furtive way he moved made the cook suspicious. He opened the cookhouse door and saw Trubec heading down the trail into town, the one that led past the Wakeford place. He shrugged his shoulders and went back to kneading bread dough. His hands froze, however, as a thought crossed his mind. He had seen the way Trubec looked as Miz Wakeford and the remarks he made when Levi wasn't around. She was all alone over there with her wee ones. McInnis dusted off his hands and reached for his coat. He had to find Levi.

Jenny stood on the back porch, her nose filled with the smell of wet wool. Her small hands, red with the cold, wrung a heavy shirt and she held above the tin tub setting on the bench. With a final twist, she added it to a pile of rinsed clothing. The brisk wind blew tendrils of her thick hair into her eyes and her skirts billowed about her legs.

With a small sigh, Jenny bent to pick up the pile of wet clothes. She had a rope line strung from the house to a tall pine in the yard. She fastened the pants to the line with wooden pins her father had made and tied the sleeves of the shirts together over the line to keep them from blowing away. She dried her stiff hands on her apron and paused for a moment to look out across the fields. Little patches of snow clung to the corner fence posts and the brown earth poking through half frozen puddles awaited Levi's plow. His work at the lumber camp was almost finished. Another week and he would be home for good which meant she wouldn't have to sleep in an empty bed any longer. Blood rushed to her cheeks with the thought.

She returned to the house. Carl was teaching Blanche to play patty-cake. The baby squealed with delight as he raised her chubby arms over her head. Jenny smiled at the scene. She would miss Carl next year when he went to school with the other children. Such a good natured child. She pressed her hand to the familiar swelling below her waist. Early October she thought. She hoped the next baby would be as good as these two.

She scooped up the laughing children, one under each arm, kissing the soft curls of each. She deposited Carl on a chair and held the baby on her lap as she spread apple butter on thick slices of bread.

A knock at the door startled her. She hadn't heard a wagon. Who could it be? Cradling the baby on her hip, she opened the door.

"Howdy, Jenny," Herman Trubec stood leaning against the door frame. Her nose crinkled at the unclean smell of him.

"Levi's not here," she said, making a move to close the door. Trubec's hand shot out above her head pushing it open farther.

"Didn't come to see Levi," his mocking eyes traveled over her rigid body.

"What *do* you want, then?" Jenny stood her ground.

"Why, I just came to say good-bye." He smiled his broken tooth smile and stepped closer. "Camp will be closing soon and you might not see me for some time."

"That's fine with me," Jenny inadvertently stepped back as she felt Carl clinging to her skirts. "You'd better not let Levi find out you're coming around here when he's not home."

"You think I care what the mealy-mouthed man of yours thinks?" As he pushed passed her, Jenny smelled whiskey on his breath.

"Carl, take the baby into the bedroom for her nap." Jenny said, putting the infant in the small boys arms. Reluctantly, he obeyed.

Picking up a rolling pin from the table, Jenny faced him. "Now, Trubec, I'll thank you to get out of my house."

"Not before I get me a little good-bye kiss." he strode purposefully toward her, one hand clamping her wrist tightly until she dropped the pin and the other pulling her to him.

"Never!" she spat at him. Twisting from his grasp, she ran for the open door.

His hands closed around her waist as she tried to step off the porch. He turned her around and with his eyes glittering, he lowered his thick lips to hers. His eyes flew open in surprise as her knee came up. She broke from his grasp and fled towards the barn. His curses ringing in her ears.

As she flew down the path her heel slipped on a frozen puddle and she found herself sprawled on her back. Casting a quick look over her shoulder she saw Trubec, still bent over, coming towards her. She jumped to her feet pulling her muddied skirts about her and ran toward the barn door. Slamming it shut, she looked wildly around for something to protect herself. Her eyes fell on a pitchfork stuck in the hay. She stood trembling, with her back against the horses stall, holding it in front of her.

"That wasn't nice, Jenny," Trubec stood blinking in the doorway. His voice a menacing growl, "Look's like I'm going to have to teach you some manners."

He stopped momentarily when he saw the pitchfork. "You goin' to try and stick me with that?" His laughter echoed through the barn.

"Come any closer and you'll see," she stood stiffly poised but he was too quick for her and in one move he pulled the fork from her hands and flung it aside. His big hands closed around her forcing her down, down onto the floor of the barn. Jenny got one hand free and raked it across his sneering face.

"Always knew you were a wild one," Trubec laughed. He held both of her arms above her head with one beefy paw while his other hand fumbled with her skirts. She tried to twist away from his seeking hands but it only made him hold her tighter.

"Stop it. Trubec! Levi will kill you!" Jenny spat at him. Disgust was giving away to real fear as he tore at her petticoat.

"Let him try," Trubec growled trying to force his lips on hers, his fowl breath smothering her. "He's no match for me. Let me show you what a real man is like."

At first, Trubec didn't see the shadow in the open door behind him but a guttural sound brought his head up. His breath caught as he looked into the cold opaque eyes of the enraged Levi coming at him.

"Didn't mean no harm," he whined, trying to get to his feet, "Jenny, she led me out here."

Jenny scrambled to her feet with relief but when she looked into her husband's face she gasped. This was not the Levi she knew but some frightening monster. He picked Trubec up like a rag doll smashing his head against the wall again and again. Blood ran down the man's face into his matted beard and his eyes rolled back as Levi continued to thrust him forward. The barn filled with dull squishing sounds.

"Levi! stop!" Jenny cried out, clutching at his arms frantically. "Let him go!"

At last, he seemed to hear her and slowly let Trubec drop to the barn floor. He stood blinking, his arms limp at his sides.

"Levi! Say something!" Jenny hugged him to her begging him to respond. Slowly his arms began to tighten around her and she felt a shudder pass through him. As they stood silently holding each other they did not notice one of Trubec's swollen eyes had opened. His hand furtively reached for the fallen pitchfork.

"Levi, look out!" Jenny had caught the movement in the corner of her eye but the warning was to late. The prongs found their mark in Levi's shoulder. He pushed his wife aside and turned to face the battered Trubec. The man lunged at him with the dripping pitchfork but his swollen eyes made him miss his mark. Levi stepped back, flinging his arm up to ward off the next blow.

He lost his balance as the prongs tore his shirt and Levi found himself falling backwards. As he hit the floor he reached around in the hay and found the handle of his axe leaning against the stall. Trubec closed in, the pitch fork ready for a final plunge into his enemy's chest. At the last moment, however, Levi twisted away and the fork stuck quivering in the floor. Levi swung the axe from a half sitting position. Trubec threw up his hand and stumbled backwards. Dazed, he looked to the floor where two of his fingers lay. Slowly, he collapsed in a heap.

Jenny never knew how she got through the next hour. Levi's shoulder was badly wounded and she knew she must tend him but Trubec lay on the floor his life's blood oozing from bloody stumps. She couldn't let him die. She knelt down and quickly, made a tourniquet from her apron to stop the flow.

"We've got to get him to the house," Jenny shouted at her husband, who sat in a daze holding his shoulder. Levi looked uncomprehendingly at his wife. "Levi! help me!" The big man slowly got to his feet. Together they carried the still body of Trubec to the cabin.

Much later that night, after McInnis and others from the camp had come for Truabec and had taken him to the doctor Levi and Jenny sat on the edge of the bed in silence.

"You saved his life after what he tried to do to you." Levi stared down at his hands.

"Lord knows I didn't care if he died but all I could think of was what they might do to you. Maybe send you to prison," Jenny placed her small hands over his. "I couldn't bear that."

"I know, I know." Levi raised his tortured eyes to his wife. "The last time I wasn't so lucky."

"The last time?" Jenny's eyes searched his, frightened at what she might see there, "Tell me what happened."

Levi's voice, barely above a whisper, began. . . .

"It was back in Albany when I lived with my Uncle Seth and Aunt Martha on their farm. One Saturday night I went into town with Judd Stockard and his brother Willis. We thought we was real growed up men. Judd and I wanted to play pool but Willis said we should have a drink first. We went into a saloon called the Fancy Lady. None of us ever tasted real whiskey before. I didn't much like the way it burned my throat and I could see Judd's eyes watering but Willis downed his with one gulp and ordered another. Judd and I didn't want to look like greenhorns so we ordered another drink too. I ain't sure how many we had. All I can remember is everything seemed strange and kinda far away." Levi's voice faded and he sat staring ahead into his memories.

"So you got drunk." Jenny said with relief, "I've seen Pa and Frank like that lot's of times."

"That wasn't all of it," Levi's husky, faltering, voice continued. "Willis got loud and started arguing with some stranger at the bar. Judd and I tried to get him to leave but Willis was a hothead and determined to get into a fight. First thing I knowed, Willis had knocked the stranger down. After that, everyone in the saloon started brawlin'. I wasn't much of a fighter and Judd not much better but we was holdin' our own and trying to get out of the place when I looked over and seen Willis laying on the floor, all doubled over. This big man was kicking him in the back with his hobnail boots. Willis wasn't moving and I saw the man pull back to aim a kick at his head. I remember grabbing him from behind but after that it's all kinda hazy. The next thing I knowed I was in a jail cell. They said I killed the man.

"You couldn't remember what happened?" Jenny's voice quivered with disbelief.

"I figured it was the whiskey."

"That's why you never...."

"Haven't had a drop since."

"Did they keep you in jail? What happened?"

Levi stared down at his big hands clenched before him and continued. "Judd ran and fetched my Uncle Seth and he got me a lawyer. There was a hearing before a judge.

Judd took the stand and told them how I was trying to save Willis. The judge was a friend of my Uncle Seth and he let me go. Gave me probation cause I'd never been in trouble before.

Jenny's small hands reached for Levi's callused ones. "It wasn't your fault."

"Truth of the matter is, I don't rightly know. They say I just kept beatin' on him." Levi turned tortured eyes to his wife. "I just can't remember."

"It was a long time ago," Jenny spoke softly, "Is that why you left Albany?"

Levi nodded, "The man I killed was named Kinross and he came from a big family of trouble makers. Uncle Seth figured I'd better leave town so the next morning I was long gone with my team before sun up. Kept on going until I got to Michigan."

"I know you didn't mean to kill that man," Jenny patted his arm, "Why, you're the most gentle man I ever knowed."

"Jen, I've tried to be a god-fearing man and not let the evil in me take over but when I saw Trubec with you, it happened all over again. It's like a bright cloud covering my eyes."

"But, Levi, you saved me from the awful man," Jenny shuddered at the memory. "Maybe losing a couple fingers will make him think twice before he tries something like that again."

"When I think of what he was trying to do, I guess I'd go after him again." His tortured eyes, a familiar blue now, searched hers. "The thing that scares me is, I can't recollect any of it. What if I get riled up over somethin' and hurt you or one of the children?"

"That just won't happen," Jenny assured him, "You love me and the children and you couldn't do us any harm." She pulled the big man to her bosom.

"She rocked him gently as she would one of her babes. It was just as well he couldn't see her troubled eyes. The memory of Levi's face, contorted in rage would haunt her for some time and she prayed she'd never see that look in his eyes again.

CHAPTER TWELVE

Josephine and Dehlia LaBlanc sat on the porch enjoying the warm rays of the late afternoon sun. They were carefully peeling potatoes. Josephine's hands, once small and delicate, were now knarled and misshapen with arthritis. She awkwardly maneuvered the small paring knife slowly.

"The crop is really bad this year," Dehlia said holding up a small potato with dark spots.

"It's the blight again," Josephine sighed, "Do the best you can." She reached into the gunnysack at her feet for another and looked at her youngest daughter. Her straight brown hair was pulled back in a tight braid. A frown wrinkled her plain face as she intently worked at salvaging another potato. She didn't have the beauty of her sister Jenny or was she quick as Marie but she was a hardworking girl, always trying to please. Often she would be in the fields helping her father and brother with the crops. One day some young farmer would take notice and realize what a catch she was. Josephine sighed. Yes, someday her youngest daughter would leave home too.

"Someone's coming." Dehlia said, looking down the road at a great cloud of dust as the sound of hoofs came nearer. "They're sure in a big hurry."

The women watched with interest a horse and rig came bouncing into the barn yard. As it neared Josephine recognized her oldest grandson, Homer. He pulled the horse to a halt and jumped down waving frantically. They hurried toward him. At eleven he was taller than his grandmother and his aunt.

"What brings you in such a state, Homer?" Josephine asked noting the boy's troubled face, "What's wrong?"

"It's Ma," Homer blurted excitedly, "Pa says you'd better come right away."

"Is the baby coming?" Josephine asked anxiously.

"She's been having pains since last night." Homer nodded, "It doesn't usually take that long. Pa's worried something ain't right."

"Dehlia, get my things." she called over her shoulder as she climbed up on the buckboard. The girl returned quickly with her mother's shawl, bonnet and small bag.

"Should I come with you?" Dehlia asked anxiously.

"No, you stay and fix supper for Pa and Frank." Josephine grabbed her bonnet, "Come on boy, let's get movin'!" Homer snapped the reins and they were off with a gallop.

Josephine looked out of the corner of her eye at the boy. He was clutching the reins and urging the old horse to the limit. Tall and thin, he was the image of his father. She thought about her son-in-law. He was a strange, quiet man. Always polite but never smiling. Not like her husband George, who always had a wink and loved a good story. Who would have thought Levi could have cut off Herman Trubec's fingers. Not that he didn't deserve it, but Levi seemed like such an even tempered man. It was hard to imagine him out of control. There were times when Josephine thought he was a might strict with the children but he did his best to provide for his family and Jenny never complained. Too bad they had never found water on the property for a well. Josephine's thoughts went ahead to her daughter. She'd never had trouble birthin' her babies before. Something had to be wrong.

When they pulled into the barnyard Levi ran down the steps of the house to meet them. Josephine had never seen him so worried. "Jenny's in a bad way," he said helping his mother-in-law down from the wagon. "I think the baby is turned wrong and I don't know how to help her."

They hurried into the house. Josephine was vaguely aware of the white faced children standing on the porch. "Please help Mama," a tearful Carl was tugging at her skirt.

"Don't worry boy," she said gently pushing him aside, "I'll take care of her."

Stepping into the bedroom, Josephine saw her daughter's pale face ravaged in pain and fear clutched her.

"I'm glad you're here, Mamman," Jenny smiled weakly up at her. "The baby just don't want to come."

"There, there, Mon Petite," Josephine brushed the damp hair back from her face, "I'll help you." She held her daughter's hand as another savage pain racked her body. When it subsided she lifted the patchwork quilt and felt the swelled body of her daughter. Levi was right. The baby was not positioned right. "I'm going to the kitchen to make you some strong tea," she said patting her hand, "I'll be right back."

"She's plumb tuckered out," Josephine strode purposefully across the kitchen to a teakettle simmering on the stove. She filled the metal tea ball with green leaves and poured boiling water over it into the tea pot. "Got to build up her strength before I try to turn the baby." she said, carrying a full mug back to Jenny.

Josephine sat on the edge of the bed waiting for a shuddering spasm to pass. "Drink this down, girl." she said holding the cup to her lips. Jenny tried to sip but was too weak and the hot liquid ran down her chin. Josephine slid her arm around Jenny's shoulders, propping her up and urged her to try again.

"It tastes good," Jenny smiled weakly at her mother, "This baby is so stubborn. I can't seem to push it out."

"I believe the baby's turned," Josephine told her, "I'm going to see if I can move it." She held her daughter as another pain engulfed her.

Jenny's body was drenched in sweat and her dark shadowed eyes pleaded, "Hurry, Mamman." she gasped.

Josephine knew what had to be done but with her crippled hands she could not help her. With a desperate look at her daughter's pale face, she turned and shouted, "Get Beatrice in here!" Levi hurried from the room and soon returned with a terrified child.

"Come here girl," Josephine ordered, "You'll have to help me."

"I don't know how," she wailed as her father thrust her forward.

"Just do as I tell you." Josephine urged, "You're hands are small and strong. You can reach in and help your mama."

"I don't want to," Beatrice cried out against her grandmother's tight grip.

"Do you want your mother to die?" Josephine said sternly.

The girl looked at her mother's pale face. "What do I have to do?" she asked in a quiet voice.

Under Josephine's direction, Beatrice's small hands probed and pushed and finally she felt the baby turn. Jenny moaned weakly and the infant, at last, came forth. Beatrice jumped back, wide eyed. Josephine lifted the child from it's mother and have it a sharp slap on the bottom. She was rewarded with a loud wail. Nodding with satisfaction, she lay her newest child on the bed next to his mother, tied the throbbing umbilical cord, and cut it.

"Thank you Mamman," Jenny's quiet voice came from the bed.

"Don't thank me," Josephine said, patting her hand. "Beatrice was the one that helped you." she said, turning to see the frightened girl still standing at the end of the bed staring.

"You have a new brother, Beatrice," Josephine smiled at her. "Do you want to be the first to hold him?"

"NO!" she screamed, turning and running from the room past her startled father.

The baby continued to cry in a surprisingly loud voice, "Didn't seem to hurt his lungs none." Levi said taking the small bundle from his mother-in-law so that she could see to Jenny. He turned to the doorway where the other children were gathered. "Meet your new brother, Abner." he said holding the newborn up so they could see him.

"He looks like a mad rooster," one of the children said and Levi had to admit, looking at the tiny face with red hair standing on end, there was a resemblance.

CHAPTER THIRTEEN

Spring 1904

Jenny looked down the church pew, checking to make sure all the children were behaving. Clayton, the youngest sat on her lap. Victor sat next to her. She reached over to smooth Abner's cowlick. The boy's hair always seemed to stand on end. She frowned as she saw his small hand reach over and pinch the unsuspecting Blanche. A sharp tug to the ear brought a surprised look to his face, quickly followed by hurt and innocence. A stern frown from Levi and he sat up folding his hands between his short legs.

They were attending the wedding of Jenny's sister, Dehlia to Marcel Patoux. Dehlia did not have the beauty of her two older sisters and Jenny had wondered if she would ever marry. Today, however, she stood proudly beside her new husband.

"I'm so happy for you," Jenny hugged her sister, "Just think, we'll be neighbors." The Pattoux farm lay between Wolverine and the Wakeford's, barely three miles away.

"So my little sister is going to be another farmer's wife," Marie said, giving Dehlia a small peck on the cheek. Her wide brimmed hat tied under the chin with turquoise tulle and a long feather to match, left no doubt Marie was a stylish city woman.

"What's wrong with being a farmer's wife?" Jenny asked pointedly. "By the way Marie, where is Harold? You're husband's not sick is he?"

"No, no, Harold is fine," she replied turning her critical gaze on her older sister. "He was much to busy to get away."

"I'm glad to hear his plumbing business is doing so well," Jenny smiled at her sister's pale silk gown, the color of cornflowers. She nervously smoothed her faded cotton dress and brushed a curl back under her ten year old bonnet.

"Oh my yes," Marie's eyes flashed with pride, "Everyone in Detroit is having bathtubs with running water put in their houses."

"Imagine that." Jenny said with wonder thinking of how they still had to carry water from the river.

"Your family is growing up," Marie said looking over at Homer and Roy who were almost as tall as Levi. "And Beatrice, what a beauty she's become." she said smiling at the girl who blushed with pleasure.

"You have your mother's hair and your father's blue eyes." She touched the girl's cheek with a gloved finger, "Soon you'll have all the young men's heads turning."

"That will be some time off." They hadn't heard Levi's quiet approach.

"I'm almost thirteen," Beatrice defiant chin came up.

"When are you and Harold going to start a family, Marie?" Levi said ignoring his daughter.

"We surely would like to have children but the lord hasn't seen fit to bless us," Marie said, quietly, "I so wish I had a daughter like Beatrice." She smiled fondly at the girl, her hand resting on her thick red curls. "Why don't I take her back to Detroit with me for a visit?"

"Jenny and Levi exchanged glances. "The girl is too young to be going off to the city." Levi said flatly.

"But Papa," Beatrice begged, "I'm a big girl. Please let me go home with Aunt Marie."

"It's out of the question." Levi said curtly. Turning on his heel, he strode towards George and Frank LaBlanc.

"I'm sorry, Jenny. I didn't mean to start trouble," Marie said. "but, I do wish you'd reconsider I'd love to have her stay with me for the summer."

"Mama, please ask Papa to let me go." Beatrice pleaded.

"That's enough," Jenny cautioned her, "Abner has to use the privy. Take him and Victor. The girl's eyes flashed in rebellion.

"Do as your Mamma says, now." Marie smiled down at her niece with a wink. "I'll talk to her." Beatrice grabbed the small hands of her brothers and trudged off with disgust.

"Marie, I wish you wouldn't fill her head with such nonsense," Jenny chided her sister, "It's not right to tease her that way."

"I'm not teasing, Jen," Marie told her earnestly, "I would love to have her come home with me. Why I bet the child has never even seen electric lights."

"That's true, Jenny shrugged, not wanting to admit she had only seen them once herself. "But, Levi will never allow it."

"You wrote me Levi let Homer go away to work in a lumber camp last winter," Marie argued, "My beautiful home in Detroit is certainly better than that." Marie reached for her sister's hand, "I'd take such good care of her."

Jenny studied the face of her younger sister. She was serious. It would be a wonderful opportunity for Beatrice. "I can't promise anything, but I'll speak to Levi."

"What's the matter, Levi?" Frank asked looking at his brother-in-law. "You look like a storm cloud."

"It's that high-falutin' sister of yours." Levi's eyes flashed with anger. "She wants to take my oldest girl back to the city with her."

"I don't see what you're so upset about," Frank shrugged, "Marie don't have any young-uns of her own. She might be good for the girl. Teach her some manners."

"What are you sayin' Frank?" Levi's voice was cold.

"Frank don't mean no harm," George interrupted, "It's just we all know what a rip-snorter she's always been. I remember when she strung one of the boys up in the barn and told him she was goin' to skin him like a hog." George chuckled.

"It's true," Levi admitted, "She's always been a handful but I'm not sure showing her city ways will make her any better. I don't want her getting uppity like Marie."

"Tell you what," Frank said, "I plan to go to Detroit myself in a month or so on business. If you let her go with Marie I'll fetch her home when I come back."

"I'll think about it," Levi said, closing the subject. "Have you seen John Faraday?" he said looking around.

"I seen him earlier talking to Hiram Lewis," George said, "You still trying to talk him into building a new school?"

"I surely am." Levi replied, "That old school is ready to fall down and I don't want it to happen while any of my young-uns are in there."

"They say there ain't any money for a new school," George said, spitting in the dirt from a wad of tobacco in his cheek.

"They been sayin' that for years," Levi muttered, "I aim to find out why. His hard blue gaze searched the different knots of people in the church yard. "We can't even get a decent teacher to come here anymore."

"As I heard tell," Frank chuckled, "You escorted the last one to the train on the end of your boot."

"He wasn't much of a teacher and he had no call to lay a whip on my Abner." Levi admitted, "If we had a new school we might be able to get good one that could learnt our children the right way."

"There's John Farady over there." Frank said pointing across the yard. "Lot's of luck," he called to Levi as he purposefully stode toward the head of the school board.

"You still fretting about my sister, Marie," Jenny asked as they rode home in silence.

"No, I was thinking about that stubborn fool of a man, John Faraday," Levi muttered. "He says they can't afford to build a new school. All they're planning to do is fix the roof."

"That school was ready to fall down when my sisters went there," Jenny agreed, "Surely they must have some money after all these years."

"I'm sure they do and they just might have to build a new one, like it or not." Levi muttered.

Jenny looked closely at her husband from under her bonnet. He was staring ahead, his eyes squinting. She had seen that look before. He was planning something. She hoped it wasn't going to cause trouble.

After much pleading on Beatrice's part and assurances by Marie that she would watch over her, the girl was at last, allowed to return to Detroit with her aunt. She boarded the train dressed in her best white blouse and blue serge shirt. Jenny blinked back tears as she waived to her daughter. She looked up to see Levi making a great show of blowing his nose. Their oldest daughter was going away from home for the first time and they both felt the loss.

"We're going to have so much fun," Marie said patting her niece's hand to reassure her as they sat back in the red plush seats. "We'll take the street car down town and have ice cream sodas at Saunder's drug store."

"I can't wait, Aunt Marie," Beatrice turned from the window, dry-eyed. "How soon will we get there?"

It was several weeks after the wedding that Jenny looked out the window as a jagged streak of lightning lit up the sky. A fierce summer storm threatened. She wished Levi and the boys would get home. They had gone to the far pasture to check on cattle but that was hours ago. It was nearly dark and still they hadn't returned.

A loud rumble of thunder told her the storm was getting closer. The baby whimpered in her arms and Victor clung to her skirts.

"Abner! get down from there," Jenny admonished her young son as he climbed atop a stack of books setting in the corner. Levi had brought them home while work was being done on the school roof. It was a good thing too. They might have been ruined in this storm.

The storm had passed through by the time Levi and boys returned. Jenny assumed they had found a dry place to wait it out but as they entered she smelled a strong odor. "Where have you been?" she looked from one to the other. They all avoided her glance. "Why do you smell of smoke?"

"It was the school house. It caught fire," Homer told her. "We seen it from the pasture."

"Oh my, what a shame," Jenny's hands flew to her mouth in surprise, "Do you think it was the lightning?"

"Could have been," Levi said hanging his hat on a peg. "That was a bad storm."

"Were you able to save it?"

"Nope," Roy smiled, "It burned right to the ground."

"I suppose they'll have to build a new school now." Jenny said staring at her husband's back. "Sure was a good thing you brought all the school books here for safe keeping."

As her husband turned to face her, Jenny, hands on her hips, raised her eyebrows.

"Just pure luck." he said, a hint of a smile playing around his lips as he turned to the tin basin to wash the grime from his hands.

CHAPTER FOURTEEN

"Do you think we'll have enough jars?" Jenny asked, wiping the corner of her apron across her forehead. She stood in the steamy LaBlanc kitchen. The pungent smell of boiling peaches filled her nostrils. Rows of fruit jars covered the table. More were lined up on the floor.

"There should be enough for this last batch," Mrs. LaBlanc said over her shoulder as she stirred a large iron kettle on the cook stove.

"What on earth do you suppose the men were thinking of when they bought a whole wagon load of ripe peaches?" Jenny said, shaking her head.

"It was Frank's idea." Mrs. LaBlanc said. "He got them for a good price at the Wolverine depot and thought he could sell then in Afton and Onaway and make money."

"Sounds like another of Frank's get rich schemes, but what I don't understand is how he talked Levi and Pa into helping him." Jenny sighed as she tightened another lid on a full jar. "All they ended up with was a wagon full of mush and pits. If we hadn't put up the rest in preserves, they would have lost the whole thing."

"Well, we should have plenty of fruit to last all winter," Mrs. LaBlanc said cheerfully," And Frank meant well."

"Him and his big ideas," Jenny frowned. "He's always making plans that don't work out. Just like how he talked Levi and I into letting Marie take Beatrice home with her. He said he'd bring her back in a couple weeks. Its been over two months and she's still there."

"What are you worried about?" her mother asked, "You know Marie will take good care of the girl."

"I don't like the sound of the letters I've been getting. Marie is spoiling her, taking her to fancy places and buying her clothes."

"Maybe you're afraid she won't want to come home." Mrs. LaBlanc's knowing brown eyes looked over her spectacles at her daughter.

"She has no choice. She is too young to be away from home and Levi would never stand for it." Jenny answered, her chin set high. "As soon as harvest time is over, Levi will go and fetch her." Secretly, she had to admit it had been a pleasant uneventful summer without the willful Beatrice starting fights or throwing tantrums. She missed her, however. Perhaps, she saw some of her own spirit in her. The rest of the Wakeford children were mostly quiet like their father. They did their chores without much complaining.

There was always Abner, of course. Jenny could not think of him without shaking her head. He had come into the world screaming and to her knowledge, there had been very few quiet moments since. His thick red curls had several cowlicks and stood up in sharp peaks. The nickname Rooster had stuck with him. As though he knew his mother was thinking of him, he burst through the door, howling. Jenny turned to see what was wrong and saw two bruises rising amid thick freckles under his eyes. She pulled him to her and placed a wet cloth on his face.

"What happened, this time?" Jenny asked over her shoulder. Carl and Blanche both tried to talk at once.

"We was jumping in the hay in the barn and Rooster said he could jump higher," A breathless Blanche began.

"He climbed way up in the loft," Carl gestured, his arms waving. "I told him to come down but he jumped anyway and hit his face on his knees."

Jenny carefully examined her son's eyes. They would be black for sure, but he didn't seem to be injured otherwise. "All of you, sit down on the porch and stay there!" she commanded.

"Here," Mrs. LaBlanc turned with a huge cookie jar, "Maybe these will make you feel better." The children thrust their hands into the molasses cookies. Abner's hand momentarily caught as he tried to pull two large cookies through the opening at once.

"Now, now, Abner," His grandmother chided him gently as his face puckered up again. "Take one at a time. That's better. Now, if you're real good and stay on the porch, I'll bring you some buttermilk later."

The children quickly sat on the top step of the porch eagerly awaiting the promised treat.

"That boy is caution." Mrs. LaBlanc said shaking her head. His mother nodded in agreement.

The last jar of peaches had been taken from the oven and the pans of peelings had been removed for the pigs when Jenny and her mother finally sat down for a cup of tea.

"Frank says he's going down to Detroit as soon as he and Pa finish haying." Mrs. LaBlanc said taking a long sip. "He'll most likely bring Beatrice home with him and Levi won't have to go."

"Is he still talking about going to California?" Jenny asked, noting the worried look on her mother's face.

"Yes, and I'm afraid he means it this time. If he can make plans with this friend of his he's seein' in Detroit, they'll take the train out West the first of the year."

"Frank has been saying things about leaving home for years," Jenny scoffed, "It's probably just talk."

"I don't know what will become of us if he goes." Mrs. LaBlanc blinked back a tear. "Your Pa is getting too old to take of the farm by himself."

"Don't fret, Mamman," Jenny said, patting her hand, "You know Levi and the boys will come over and now that Dehlia is married, Marcel can help to."

"I wouldn't count on that one," her mother pursed her lips, "From what I've seen, Marcel spends more time in town drinkin' and playin' cards than taking care of his farm. Dehlia is doing most of the chores."

"She seems happy enough," Jenny said lifting the fussing Clayton from the floor and absently unbuttoning her blouse for the baby to nurse. He sucked noisily, his yellow curls damp with the effort.

"Dehlia's not one to complain," Mrs. LaBlanc sighed, "Especially when she thought she would never get a husband." She glanced around to make sure the children could not hear. "I'll tell you something, Pa and I were more than a little surprised when Marcel proposed."

"Well, maybe he saw what a good woman Dehlia was," Jenny said, "Not like those *others* he ran around with in town."

"I never said this to anyone before," her mother quietly confided, "We heard Marcel's folks gave him one last chance to behave himself. Promised him a farm if he settled down and got married. Not that it's worth much, but I guess when Dehlia said she'd have him, that settled it."

"Maybe he'll settle down now that he has Dehlia," Jenny said, "I'm sure she loves him."

"Well, she's made her bed and will have to make the best of it." Mrs. LaBlanc sniffed, "I was hoping she would find a good man like Levi to take care of her but they're not many around like him."

"Yes, Levi is very special."

"He hasn't had anymore of his spells, has he?" Mrs. LaBlanc looked closely at her daughter.

"Of course not," Jenny replied, "You know what Trubec was trying to do when Levi went after him years ago."

"I didn't mean anything like that," Mrs. LaBlanc assured her. "It's just that there are times when Levi seems, I don't know how to say it, like he's thinking of something far away and don't know what's going on around him."

"Levi's always been a quiet man. It's hard for him to say what's on his mind." Jenny said but she did not meet her mother's eyes. She could not bring herself to tell her of the times Levi disappeared alone into the woods and how his eyes sometimes had such a haunted look. Whatever his private devils were, he would not share them with anyone.

"Levi's a good husband and a wonderful father," Jenny said staunchly.

"Of course he is," Her mother agreed, "Of course he is."

CHAPTER FIFTEEN

Levi sat stiffly on the red plush seat of the Michigan Central heading south. It was his first train ride and the swaying made him slightly nauseous. His brother-in-law, Frank, puffing a cigar, lounged comfortably gazing out the window. "Ain't this the life?" he gestured grandly, "We must be moving at least, fifteen miles an hour."

"How long did you say it would take to get to Detroit?" Levi eyed Frank wondering why the motion didn't seem to bother him.

"We have to make a couple stops and change trains in Durand but I calculate we should be there come morning."

Levi took out his pocket watch. "If we're on time, I should be able to pick up Beatrice and catch the afternoon train home."

"You'll have plenty of time. Still don't know why you thought you had to come fetch her yourself," Frank admonished," I'd have brought her back with me in a couple weeks."

"The girl's been down here long enough," Levi's lips were set in a firm line, "She's needed at home."

"Suit yourself," Frank nodded agreeably, "But you should stay in Detroit a few days and see the sights. I hear tell they got electric lights in some of the houses now."

"I seen big cities before," Levi grumbled, "They ain't nothin' but trouble."

He turned to stare out the dusty window, watching empty farm land go by. Only an occasional field of corn stalks broke the monotony. They stopped to pick up passengers in Gaylord and the miles again clicked by.

"Yes sir, this is the way to travel." Frank said, stretching out his legs. He was thoroughly enjoying himself. "Can't wait until I'm on my way to California."

"You really planning to leave your folks and go out west?" Levi said studying his brother-in-law with disbelief. He'd never understood this stocky farm boy and his farfetched ideas.

"Yep, this time I got it all worked out," Frank flicked the ash of his cigar on the floor. "This friend of mine, Jim Wells, just got back from out west." Frank looked around to made sure no one was in ear shot. "I'm meeting him tomorrow." Leaning closer, he whispered, "He's got himself a map to a silver mine. He says we'll be rich in six months."

"And where would you be gettin' the money to get out there?" Levi asked pointedly.

"Paw said I can have my share of the money from the corn crop."

"That won't buy you much more than a train ticket," Levi scoffed, "What you goin' to live on?"

"Don't you worry none about ole' Frank. My friend Jim has a stake. With his money and my smart head for sums we'll be on easy street in no time." Frank sat back puffing confidently on his cigar.

Levi clamped his jaw shut in silence. Some of Frank's previous wild ideas came to mind. There was a time when he went up to Ontanogen to work the copper mines. He was sure he'd get rich there, too. He'd stuck it out three months and came home. Levi tipped his hat over his eyes and leaned back trying to get some sleep. Pictures of Jenny and the children filled his mind and he wished, fervently, he was home in his own bed.

The train chugged into the Michigan Central depot at Eight fifteen the next morning. Levi rose stiffly. Frank grabbed his valise.

Levi looked around him as they stepped down from the train. The engine sat, several cars down, puffing like a tired giant. He followed his brother-in-law through the bustling depot trying not to show his amazement at the throngs of people hurrying about.

"We have to walk to Michigan Avenue to catch the streetcar," Frank gestured towards the tall glass doors, deftly avoided a redcap steering a cart full of luggage. As they crossed the marble floor of the depot sun shone down from the high windows on polished wooden benches. Levi looked about him in wonder. People were hurrying everywhere.

Mothers clutching purse strings, their children hanging on their skirts. Important looking men carrying various sizes of suitcases strode purposefully past them. He followed Frank out the tall doors to the streets of Detroit.

Across the street from the depot was a large green park. They took a path through it to the trolley stop. Soon a car attached to strange looking wires stopped before them. He watched Frank hand the conductor a nickel and he fished one out of his pocket to do the same. He barely had time to sit on the rattan seat before the car took off. He was amazed at how fast and smooth it ran.

"Will you look at that!" Frank was gesturing out the window. Traveling next to the streetcar was a strange looking cart moving along without being pulled by a team. "Must be one of those horseless carriages."

Levi stared at the weird looking vehicle. It rattled and snorted as it left the trolley behind in a puff of smoke. He wrinkled his nose at the smell coming in the window and sneezed loudly.

At Frank's direction they got a transfer and boarded another streetcar that took them down Jefferson Avenue which was near Marie's house. Between the trees they glimpsed the lush green island of Belle Isle floating on the shimmering Detroit river in the early morning sun. Large freighters moved slowly down the river. A fat ferry boat was crossing the river. Frank explained it was going to Canada just across the water on the other side.

At Frank's direction they got off at St. Clair street. Levi followed him down a shady street to a large two story home with a tiny yard. They walked up the steps and across the porch and knocked on the stained glass door.

"Well, look who's here," Marie smiled nervously as she opened the door. "I didn't expect to see you in the city, Levi."

"Come to get my girl," Levi said, gruffly, "Her maw needs her at home."

"So soon?" Marie fluttered as she motioned them into the cool parlor. "It seems like she just got here."

"Aunt Marie, I'm ready to go shopping." Beatrice's voice floated down the stairs. The girl's eyes flew open in surprise as she rounded the landing and saw her father standing below her.

He, in turn, could not believe his eyes.

She wore a dark green taffeta suit of the latest fashion. Her red curls were smartly pulled back under a flat brimmed black straw hat and on her feet were kidskin boots with shiny buttons. Levi stared in disbelief.

"Papa!" she cried. There was a moment's hesitation before she ran to him. Levi patted the girl stiffly as she threw her arms around him. At thirteen she was taller than Jenny. It was almost impossible for him to comprehend this stylish young woman was his tomboy daughter.

"You'd best be changing your clothes and packing up your things, girl." Levi said sternly, "We've got to catch the afternoon train."

"You mean I have to go home today?" Beatrice drew back, looking bewildered. "Aunt Marie said I could stay as long as I wanted."

"Your Aunt knows better," Levi gave his sister-in-law a cold look. "Now get your belongings."

Beatrice's blue eyes flashed at her father but the stern look on his face reduced her to familiar wailing sobs. "But, I don't want to go home!" She looked at her aunt, appealing to her for support.

"Now, Beatrice dear," Marie said placing her arms around the girl gently, "Your Papa has come all the way to Detroit for you. He says your Mamma needs you at home."

"What for?" The girls eyes, so like her fathers, blazed. "Is she having another baby?"

"That's enough," Levi's cold voice filled the room. "Get your things together in ten minutes or you'll go without them"

"She'll be all right," Marie said nervously as Beatrice fled up the stairs. "Why don't you set down a spell and let me fix you something to eat."

"Come on, Levi." Frank said, trying to smooth things. "You've got 'til this afternoon before the train leaves."

Levi hesitated. His stomach was growling. "Guess I could use a cup of coffee." he admitted sitting gingerly on the edge of an overstuffed velvet chair. Marie scurried to the kitchen.

"What do you think of Marie's house?" Frank asked gesturing at the new brocade sofa and ornate tables.

"Her husband must be doin' right well," Levi commented dryly staring at the red roses in the wallpaper with growing uneasiness. Fastened to the wall were glass fixtures with round globes and tear drops of crystal hanging down. They must be the electric lights Frank told him about.

Levi could sit no longer. He stood and paced to the lace covered windows to peer out. In the bay window stood a grand piano.

"Marie plays some." Frank said noticing his gaze. "But she never was as good as Jenny."

"Jenny knows how to play the piano?" Levi turned to Frank with surprise.

"Sure, she can. She's real good too," Frank told him, "She learned at the Mueller house on their pump organ."

"She never said nothin' to me." Levi said quietly.

"Maybe she thought you wouldn't like it." Frank shrugged, "Let's go see how Marie's coming with breakfast."

They went down the hall to a large empty kitchen. A coffee pot bubbled on the stove. They both noted the back stairway and realized Marie must have gone to talk to Beatrice.

"She better tell her not to pack any of them fancy duds. She won't have need for them at home." Levi said, his voice carrying up the stairs..

"Don't worry about it," Frank urged, "Come look at this new fangled gas stove.

"Where's the kindlin?" Levi asked looking around.

"Don't need any," Frank, who had been to his sisters before, lit a match and turned a china knob. Levi stepped back as blue flame jumped from the burner. Next, Frank opened the oak ice box and produced a bottle of cold milk. "They have it delivered to the house." he said, enjoying Levi's astonishment. Although he tried not to show it, the thing that really impressed Levi was flow of cold water from a spigot over the sink. How Jenny would love that! He stared out the window.

His thoughts plagued him. *How was he going to handle Beatrice after she'd seen all this? The sooner they left for home the better!*

Frank took two china cups from the cupboard and poured the coffee. He added milk from the cool bottle and offered a cup to Levi.

There was a plate of fresh donuts covered with a napkin on the table and Frank proceeded to help himself. Levi stirred his coffee in silence. His patience was almost gone when he heard Marie and Beatrice on the stairs. He looked up noting the girls red rimmed eyes but frowned when he saw her still wearing the taffeta dress.

"Told you not to let her wear those fancy clothes." he said turning to Marie with a scowl.

"She's outgrown all the clothes she brought with her," Marie hastily explained," And she'll need a jacket on the train."

Levi looked from Marie to the way Beatrice filled out the suit and grudging admitted she was probably right. "If that's all she's got, she can wear it but she sure won't have any use for fancy duds when she gets home." He didn't see the conspirital look his daughter gave her aunt as she followed him to the front door.

"Much obliged to you Marie, for looking after Beatrice," Levi mumbled, "Good luck to you Frank," He shook hands and they were on their way back to the train. They caught the trolley at the corner and Beatrice watched familiar sights of the trip downtown sadly. They crossed Woodward Ave. and she could see busy shoppers going into Kerns department store. She was to have gone there with her aunt today. Later they were going to Saunders for ice cream. Beatrice blinked back tears and raised her chin. Her Pa might make her go home this time but she would find a way to come back and next time she would stay!

"You sit here," Levi pointed to a place on the bench. Beatrice watched her father with a mixture of hate and despair as his tall shabby figure crossed to the ticket window.

"You know that man?" a voice startled her. She looked up. Before her, stood a stranger. A short man in a dark suit. Grey whiskers covered most of his face. Black eyes peered out from under the brim of a his hat.

"He's my Pa," Beatrice answered, "Do you know him?"

"A long time ago, back East."

Across the room, Levi looked up and saw the man staring intently at him. He turned and hurried out the side door. Beatrice watched with curiosity as the stranger strode across the station after him. Beatrice was dumbfounded. Who was this man and why was her father afraid of him?

She thought of following but her suitcase was heavy and Levi had told her to wait. It was almost time for the train to leave when the stranger returned.

"Where's your Pa?" the man asked in a menacing tone.

"He's gone back home," she lied. "He left me to catch the train to my Aunt's house up north." She'd never seen Levi run from anyone before and she wasn't about to tell this stranger anything.

"What's your name?" the man asked, his black eyes boring into hers.

"Who wants to know?" She returned his stare.

"Clyde Kinross. You tell your Pa I'll be watching for him." The man spat in a spittoon and turned away.

Looking up at the big clock on the wall, Beatrice realized her train was ready to leave. She grabbed her valise and ran for the platform. Looking frantically up and down she spotted her father between two cars. He motioned her to the next car. She boarded the train and found a seat next to the window as the conductor shouted ALL ABOARD. She clutched her bag and watched as the train left the station wondering what she would do when they asked for her ticket.

A mile out of the city Levi slid into the seat next to her. "Papa! Where have you been? Her father didn't answer. "There was a man looking for you. He said his name was Kinross."

"I know," Levi said turning to stare out the window.

CHAPTER SIXTEEN

"Whatcha doin'?" Abner stuck his freckled face through the ferns. Carl turned to frown at his young brother. He was squatted at the edge of a small stream that branched away from the larger Pigeon river. In his sturdy young hand was a long thin branch. A string attached to it dangled down near a dark pool of gently moving water.

"I'm trying to catch some brook trout," he whispered, "Be quiet or you'll scare 'em away."

"How come you get to fish on Sunday and the rest of us can't do nothin' but chores?" the smaller boy asked.

"Cause Pa knows I always bring home a batch for supper and he purely loves these little 'uns."

"Don't see no fish." Abner leaned close to his brother, peering into the dark pool.

"They're there," Carl assured him and was answered by a quick tug on the line. He pulled a small shiny brook trout from the stream. He removed the hook carefully from its mouth not to disturb the feathered fly on the end. He added it to a string of a dozen or more fish resting in the cool water.

"Let me try." Abner begged, edging closer.

"No, you're to little." Carl said, stretching out on his stomach to reach further into the stream.

"Am not!" Abner protested, making a grab for the pole. His foot slipped on the slippery stones and before Carl could grab him, he landed face down in the shallow creek. He came up sputtering and made a grab for his straw hat that was slowly floating down stream.

"Come on out of there," Carl said reaching out his hand to help him. With a tug he had the boy back on the river bank,

"Look at you," he said shaking his head, "Pa's goin' to wail you good for getting your Sunday clothes wet."

This brought a barrage of choking sobs and Carl felt sorry for him. "Quit your yellin' and give me your shirt. I'll wring it out." He twisted the shirt and gave it back to his little brother. "You'll probably dry out some afore you get home."

"I can run real fast and flap my arms," Abner said hopefully, turning around in a circle until he fell.

"Maybe nobody will notice." Carl sighed. Little brothers!

Their bare feet made small puffs dust as they walked.

"How did you find me, anyhow?" Carl asked.

"I seen you go through the pasture and I followed."

"Did you shut the gate?"

"I think so."

Carl frowned at his young brother skipping along beside him. Pa's new team of horses were in the pasture and if they got out they would both be in for it. He hurried his pace and Abner had to run to catch up. As they neared the clearing Carl looked anxiously across the pasture. His worst fears were realized when he saw the open gate. There was no sign of the horses.

"Hurry!" he cried, dropping his fish and pole. "We got to find Pa's team." The two frightened boys slid under the fence and ran to the other side. They stood staring across the empty pasture, listening.

"Come on, they're over there," Carl said, turning to run. Breaking through the thicket he stopped in horror. The horses stood next to a wild apple tree calmly gorging themselves on rotting apples. Not only would they bloat from eating the spoiled fruit but their coats were covered in burrs. It would take hours to brush them out. First, he had to get them back into the pasture. He waved his arms at the animals to no avail. The animals backed farther into the thicket.

"They won't come," Abner said clinging to his brother's shirt. "What are you goin' to do?"

"We're goin' to have to ride 'em out," Carl decided. "Come here, I'll help you up on the Bay's back."

Abner stood back shaking his head but his brother grabbed him by the seat of the pants and flung him across the broad back of the nearest horse. The little boy hung on in terror. Quickly, Carl grabbed the mane of the other one and pulled himself up on his back. After much urging with his knees and a smack on the rump with a stick, the big horse headed out of the thicket. Abner's horse followed.

They rode the animals back to the pasture and Carl jumped down to close the gate. Abner clung to the mane of his horse waiting for Carl to help him down but his brother was busy trying to pull out some of the deeply embedded burrs from his animal before he let it go.

Getting up his courage, the boy tried to slide off the horse but in so doing, his leg came in contact with a sharp burr and he let out a scream. The startled horse took off across the pasture at a gallop. Abner clung to the horses neck in panic.

Carl jumped back on his horse hoping to head him off. He had seen the pile of fence posts stacked in the corner of the field next to a bale of barbed wire and Abner's horse was heading right for it.

Levi sat on the edge of the porch watching Homer and Roy pitch horseshoes. The boys, both teenagers, worked in Wolverine during the summer. Homer at the lumber mill and Roy at a small chair factory.

They roomed together during the week but always managed to get home for their mother's cooking on Sunday.

In Levi's hands was a much read picture post card from Jenny's brother Frank. It was postmarked Twin Falls, Idaho. The simple message read: 'Dear Sister and family, We're almost to Kalifornia. Did Levi ever grow anything like this. HaHa.' On the other side was a picture of a farmer holding two giant potatoes. Each one more than filled his hands. Levi had never seen potatoes that big and it fascinated him. What a place Idaho must be to grow vegetables like that.

Inside the clatter of dishes being put away was interrupted by the door banging open as Beatrice burst through, carrying wet dishtowels. "Blanche can finish by herself. I'm not waiting all day for such a slow poke." With a huff she began tossing the towels over a small line hanging across the end of the porch.

Jenny sighed as she looked up from her rocker where she nursed the newest baby, Bernadette. "If you're done in the kitchen, why don't you go see what Victor and Clayton are up to."

"Why do I have to go?" came the familiar whine but a stern look from Levi and she reluctantly stepped off the porch in search of her younger brothers.

"I wonder how Marie is doing," Jenny mused, "Her baby is due any time now."

"I expect that rich husband of hers will have a full time servant to come and take care of her." Levi muttered, still gazing at his postcard.

"She wanted Beatrice to come and stay with her." Jenny mused, "Heaven knows, the girl has taken care of enough babies."

"Told you before, the girl's not going anywhere." Levi muttered. This was an old argument. "She belongs here at home to help you."

Jenny had to admit he was probably right but she could understand how much Beatrice wanted to go to the city. She had been telling them stories of the wonders of Detroit ever since she had gotten back home last fall. She thought of her daughter, almost fourteen. She was a real beauty with her porcelain complexion and auburn hair. She had inherited her mother's full figure too. The young men of Afton and Wolverine were already casting glances her way but so far, her sharp tongue and haughty ways had kept them a distance.

They both looked up as Beatrice came running toward the house. "Papa! come quick!"

"What is it?" Jenny cried, jumping up. "Has something happened to Victor and Clayton?"

"No, it's Carl and Abner. They're riding Pa's new horses in the pasture and they're going real fast."

"They're riding the team?" Levi's face was contorted in rage as he ran after his daughter.

Levi rounded the barn in time to see Abner clinging to his prize Bay as it raced across the pasture. The boy was screeching in terror, which made the frightened animal run faster. Carl was trying to urge the other horse to head him off. Levi watched in anger as Abner's horse headed for the pile of fence posts. At the last moment the animal saw the obstacle and veered to the left. He missed the logs but his momentum could not stop him from hitting the bale of barbed wire. The animal screamed in pain as the wire wrapped around his legs, cutting to the bone. Carl jumped down from his horse and ran. He climbed the fence and reached over to clutch his brother's shirt, pulling him from the back of the thrashing animal away from the flailing hooves. The frightened boys watched as the big animal came crashing down, the barbed wire tangled around its legs.

Levi reached the scene moments later and grasped a post hole digger laying on the ground. He lifted it high above his head and brought it down on the horse's head, putting it out of its misery.

The boys climbed down from the fence and faced their father, trembling. One look at his father's eyes, which had turned to flat grey slits and Carl began to back away. "Run Abner!" he shouted trying to push the boy behind him. But his brother stood frozen staring at his father's contorted features.

Instinctively, Carl ducked and felt the whoosh of the post hole digger swing over his head. There was a deathly thud and he looked up in time to see his brother's small body float like a limp rag and drop to the ground. Unmindful of his own danger, he ran to the boy and threw himself over his still body.

"Levi! STOP!" Jenny's voice rang out. She and the older boys had reached the scene. They stood stunned at what they saw before them. Thrusting the baby into Beatrice's arms, she ran and flung herself at Levi who had raised the post hole digger above his head, ready to swing it again. She couldn't stop him but her momentum caused him to miss his target and the post hole digger only grazed Carl's leg. Homer and Roy ran to help. One jumped on his back, the other tried to grab the post hole digger from his grasp. Levi flung them aside but then a great shudder passed through him and he stood blinking, uncomprehendingly at the sight before him while the digger slipped from his hand. Jenny knelt on the ground clutching Abner's still body to her. Carl sat rubbing his leg. Homer and Roy stood staring, warily at him. He gazed from one to another with a puzzled look. "What happened?" he asked.

"Homer, carry Abner to the house." Jenny ordered. Obeying his mother, he picked up his little brother carefully, noting the blood seeping from under his red curls.

"Carl? can you walk?" His mother asked. The boy nodded and limped along after her. No one looked at Levi standing quietly, his arms at his sides, as they all moved past him.

Homer lay Abner on the bed. The boy's breath came in small spurts. His eyes remained closed. Jenny held a wet cloth to the wound on his head. When the bleeding stopped she gently unbuttoned his clothes to remove them. Turning him on his side to slide his arm from his shirt she gasped at the ugly blue bruise on his back. It spread from his buttocks all the way up his back. She bit her lip to keep from crying out. She lay him gently back on the bed. Still he did not move.

"Should I go for the doctor?" Homer asked from the door.

"Let's wait a little while," Jenny said bathing Abner's face. "There's not much to be done until he wakes up." The other children silently stuck their heads in the room and quietly withdrew when their mother motioned them away. It was later when the lamp had been lit and shadows flickered over the small form on the bed that she heard Levi's heavy step enter the room. She heard the sharp intake of breath and a muffled groan but she did not look up. This time she could not find it in her heart to comfort her husband. Not while the still form of her son lay before her.

"Ma, Roy and me should get back to town," Homer said, standing awkwardly at the door, "But we'll stay if you need us."

"It's all right," Jenny told him, not looking up, "There's nothing you can do." The boys left and the other children, quiet for once, settled in their beds.

With strained silence the parents of Abner kept watch. She held the small limp hand and searched his white face for signs that he might waken. Dear God, what would she do if he didn't? Try as she may she could not blot out the memory of Levi standing over the boy. How could she ever forgive him?

It was almost daybreak when the boy let out a soft moan. Jenny searched his face and said a prayer of thanks when his eyes opened.

"Mamma?" said the small voice, "Tell papa I'm sorry about his horse." An anguished cry came from the corner where Levi stood vigil. His broken sobs filled the room.

CHAPTER SEVENTEEN

"It's done." Levi strode into the kitchen, slamming the door behind him. He dropped his tall frame into a chair at the head of the table.

"You've really sold the farm?" Jenny clasped a dishtowel tightly in her hands. "Did you get your price?"

"That I did, and a little more. Praise the good lord." Levi said, bowing his head to bless the meal. The children all lowered their heads in unison. He finished saying grace and helped himself from a large bowl of mashed potatoes. The children knew better than to talk at the table but their faces were bright with curiosity. Beatrice brought bowls of squash and beans and Jenny placed a platter of tender young venison before her husband. She poured milk from a sturdy pitcher into the boys cups and tea for Levi. Taking her place at the other end of the table, she buttered biscuits for Victor and Clayton. Two spots of color, the only indication of her turmoil, rose on her cheeks. She couldn't believe Levi had really sold their home. She sat staring at her plate, fighting back tears that threatened to roll down her cheeks. It was much to late to do anything about it.

Their home belonged to someone else. She swallowed a piece of meat without tasting it. There was nothing she could do.

It had all started last summer with the postcard from Frank. Levi had not stopped thinking about Idaho. It was true the crops had been getting worse each year and a chance to go to a place where potatoes grew as big as your hand had been a great temptation but Jenny could not believe he'd actually sold the farm. Thoughts of leaving her parents and going to a strange place terrified her, but, like it or not, she wouldn't say a word. Levi was her husband and if he thought it was the right thing for her and the children then she would have to make the best of it.

Within a week Levi had made arrangements for the family to take the train west. They would look for a farm in Idaho. Frank had passed through on his way to California last summer and had assured them the land was rich and the climate mild. Levi promised Jenny he would find them a new home with a good well. She had to admit, it was something to look forward to.

When they broke the news to Homer and Roy they found to their surprise the boys did not want to go.

"Levi, tell them they have to come with us," Jenny pleaded.

"The boys will be fine and they can stay and help your Pa," Levi reasoned, "We'll send for them later."

"Why do I have to go?" Beatrice pouted, "If the boys can stay I'd rather go to Aunt Marie's."

"You're going with us." Levi said, frowning at his daughter. "The boy's are almost growed and your mother needs you." Beatrice took one look at her father's face and stomped out of the room.

"How come you don't want to come with us?" Blanche followed her sister to the porch. She sat on the top step next to her older sister.

"Who would want to go to a dumb place like Idaho?" Beatrice said staring ahead.

"Uncle Frank says it's real nice there," Blanche argued. "He told Pa its warm all the time."

"Huh!" Beatrice snorted, "He's always saying things are fine and then they turn out different."

"Tell me what's it like to ride a train," Blanche said, changing the subject, "I can't wait."

"They go choo choo choo," Abner cried, banging through the door. He was followed by Victor and Clayton. The boys all began to make train sounds stomping across the porch down the steps past their sisters. The girls shook their heads in disgust.

Inside, Levi heard Abner's train imitation and winced. He still could not look at the boy without feeling pain and guilt. The boy never complained but sometimes he cried out in his sleep. When he did, Levi stared at the ceiling for hours.

Two weeks later Levi and Jenny boarded the train with eight of their ten children heading for Idaho. They decided to take only necessities with them. The children wore several layers of clothing and the rest was in two large trunks. They stored the remainder of their belongings in the LaBlanc's barn. They would send for them when they got settled.

At the station, Jenny clutched her mother and father trying in vain to hold back the tears. "Please look after Homer and Roy." her choked voice pleaded. Her tall sons stood awkwardly by, trying not to show tears to their younger brothers and sisters as they climbed excitedly on to the train and waved from the windows. The big engine puffing impatiently blew its whistle and the conductor urged them on board. Levi gently pulled Jenny from her mother and helped her up the steps. Seated with baby Bernadette in her arms she turned and waved her handkerchief out the window as the train pulled away. Her parents and sons watched as the cars grew smaller and disappeared down the track.

Victor and Clayton sat with their noses against the windows watching the fields go by. Abner hung over the seat staring at the other passengers. Carl sat holding Earl the youngest boy.

"When will we see a big city?" Blanche asked her sister as she peered out the window at endless farmland.

"We'll change trains at Durand," Beatrice told her with the air of an experienced traveler. The taffeta suit she had worn home from Detroit was straining at the seams and the shiny buttons threatened to pop but she wore it with an air of authority knowing it was store bought and not like the rest of her family in their homemade clothes.

"We're hungry, Mamma," Abner tugged at Jenny's skirts as they boarded the train for Chicago.

"Wait until we get settled in our seats," she promised, shooing them along ahead of her to their car.

As the train pulled out she reached into her large brocade bag and pulled out shiny apples. She gave one to each of the children and they munched contentedly. She gave the last one to Levi. Although her stomach growled, she could wait until they reached Chicago.

Darkness fell as the train moved past empty fields. The conductor lit small lamps at either end of the car. They swayed with the movement of the train. One by one, the children drifted off to sleep. Jenny glanced to her side and saw Levi's head nod forward. She shivered and moved closer to her husband trying to blot out fears of the unknown that awaited them.

Her hand slid down the folds of her skirts until it reached a thick lump near the pocket. Their life savings, in a small pouch, was sewn to her petticoat. Assured it was still there, she closed her eyes and tried to sleep.

They were awakened with a screech and bump as the train pulled into Chicago. The sleepy children stumbled down the steps gazing in wonder at the tall glass windows in the huge depot. Inside, they were told the train heading west would be leaving in twenty minutes on track ten. There was barely time to use the facilities before herding the children along to their next destination.

Jenny sent Levi in search of a place to buy some food. It was early and most of the shops were closed. Tempting smells led him to a small bakery where he purchased two bags of donuts and a small jug of milk.

His long legs carried him through the depot and out to the tracks just as the conductor shouted, "All Aboard." He strode through the cars until he found his family waiting for him.

"Is that all you could find?" Jenny looked with despair at the sack of oily donuts. They wouldn't last long with her starving family.

"It'll hold them until the train stops again," Levi assured her. "Then we'll eat proper." What he didn't know was that the train was an express and only stopped for water and coal until it reached Iowa.

The train chugged out of Chicago and soon left the city behind. After a time the children got tired of looking out the windows only Levi's stern gaze kept them in their seats.

"Eat your lunch Harold." Abner and Victor hung over the back of their seats staring at a large woman and her fat little boy as she tore a chunk of bread from a loaf on her lap and wrapped it around a dripping sausage she pulled from a bag. She smiled as the boy stuffed the food obediently into his mouth. She took more food for herself and licked her fingers contentedly.

"Can we have some?" Abner looked longingly at the food.

"Certainly not!" The woman stared at the freckled faced boy with revulsion. "Don't bother us or I'll call the conductor."

"Abner! Don't be troublin' the lady," Levi's tall form filled the aisle.

"But Pa, we're hungry and she's got lots of food." the boy argued.

"Go see your Ma," Levi's voice commanded. The boys slid down into the aisle and ran to their mother. Jenny broke off two small pieces from a stale donut to satisfy them.

"They didn't mean no harm, Ma'am." Levi mumbled turning away, his face flushed with embarrassment. The woman sniffed and stuffed another sausage into her mouth.

It was nearly dark when the train pulled into Davenport where they had an hour stop over. Jenny and Levi led the children from the train in search of a place to eat. Next to the depot was a small cafe. When they opened the door Jenny's knees nearly gave out as warm delicious smells greeted them.

"That's quite a brood you have there." The proprietor, a plump, rosy cheeked woman greeted them. "Looks like they could use some of my vittles." Jenny nodded gratefully as the woman led them to a long table covered with shiny blue oilcloth.

They all looked up when the door slammed open and the fat woman from the train came charging in with her red faced son in tow. "How about some service over here?" she demanded banging her fist on the table. "We have to catch a train so be quick about it."

"Yes ma'am," the owner replied, "Just as soon as I take care of these folks." Abner and Victor giggled as the woman's face grew red with rage.

"If you'd like to wash up, there's a place in back," the woman whispered to Jenny. Quickly, she and the girls followed her down a short hall to a room with a china bowl and a pitcher of warm water. They took turns making use of the privy outside and washing the grime from the train from their faces and hands.

The facilities on the train had been rudimentary. A pail of water with a ladle and a chamber pot in the corner with only a curtain for privacy. They gratefully dried their hands on a clean white towel and headed back to the table.

The family devoured plates of chicken and dumplings, mashed potatoes, and rutabagas. They topped it off with generous slices of apple pie. Before they left the cafe Levi, having learned a lesson, purchased several loaves of bread and a wheel of cheese. His family would not go hungry again. Sated, they hurried back to the train that was puffing impatiently on the tracks.

The next day the train made its way through the bleak Nebraska farmlands. It made two stops. The Wakefords gratefully got off to stretch they're legs and add to they're food supply. That night the baby was fretful and Jenny paced the car trying to soothe her crying. In the dark swaying car she tried not to think about their uncertain future, but the worries came. They didn't know a soul in Idaho. What if they needed help? Back home, they had her parents and many friends to call on. She hummed to the baby and tried to calm her fears. She would have to trust the lord. Levi had always been a good provider and he would know what to go.

The train made its way through Wyoming and they saw their first mountains. The boys fought for a place at the windows to see snow topped peaks.

Their excitement knew no bounds when the train wound its way through the mountain passes and they could see the ground fall away from the tracks in deep gorges. Blanche took a timid look as they crossed a high trestle and promptly got sick. Jenny soaked a handkerchief in cold water from the bucket and wiped the girl's face. She cleaned her jacket the best she could and told her not to look out again.

It was five in the afternoon when they finally arrived in Twin Falls. The tired family stepped down from the train onto the windswept platform.

"I thought it was supposed to be warm here," Beatrice said hugging her arms to her against the fierce wind.

"It's just night comin' on," Levi assured them, "You're Uncle Frank says we're almost to California and it never gets cold there. Now come along."

He led his family down the dimly lit streets. In the distance they could see the dark shapes of mountains hovering like sentinels.

"Is that a hotel," Jenny pointed hopefully to a large building across the street.

"Too fancy." Levi said rejecting the idea. They walked several more blocks. Just before they reached the end of the wooden sidewalk he spotted a large house with a sign reading "ROOMS" A stern faced woman with her hair pulled back in a bun stood in the doorway.

"I've go two rooms," she said curtly, "They're a dollar a night, in advance."

"Do you serve meals?" Jenny asked hopefully.

"Reckon I could fix you some supper," the woman reluctantly agreed. "That'll be twenty-five cents for grownups and fifteen for the children."

Levi blanched at the ridiculous price but looking at Jenny's exhausted face, he agreed to stay. They trudged up the steep stairs to two sparsely furnished rooms. Jenny and Levi took the bed in the largest room. The boys would have to make do on the floor. Beatrice and Blanche would share their bed with the two youngest boys, Earl and Clayton.

Levi had not planned to stay more than one night at the rooming house but he soon found out there were few places in his price range to stay. He also found to his dismay there weren't any farms in the vicinity for sale at this time. It took Levi the better part of a week before he found a house on the edge of town for rent. It wasn't much more than a shack.

Jenny stared aghast at the one room, separated by a dirty curtain. She tore her eyes from the beds with soiled mattresses to a rickety cook stove and a plank table.

"Mamma!" Beatrice stood horrified. "We can't stay here!"

"It's just for a little while until Papa can find us a place." She turned away from her daughter. "We'll just have to get busy and clean it up."

Jenny squared her shoulders and put every one to work. She sent Carl and Victor out to the shed to find firewood. Levi primed the rusty pump in the yard and finally got a yellowish trickle of water which they heated on the stove in a dented bucket. With broom and scrub brush they cleaned the best they could. They also managed to repair the outhouse that listed dangerously and had only half a door. By nightfall it was still a drafty old structure but it had been made livable for the time being.

Every morning Levi walked into town to inquire about any land for sale. He borrowed a horse from the livery stable and rode around the countryside. Every place he found was more than he could afford or it was so run down he couldn't see bringing his family to it. Night after night he came home with no news.

At Jenny's insistence, Levi bought two laying hens and a cow. Their nest egg was depleting at an alarming rate but these were necessities to feed the family. Her parents had shipped blankets and a few household items they had stored with them.

Jenny sat on a stool, nursing Bernadette, trying to keep her mind off the freezing drafts that constantly came through the cracks in the wall. The older children were enrolled in school. It was better for them to have something to do all day. Maybe Levi would find a job today. They'd given up looking for a farm until spring.

It was the first week in December when Carl, on his way to the outhouse could not get the door open. Levi came forward to help and found, after much shoving, that it was blocked with a three foot pile of snow. The wind howled and huge flakes blew in as he tried to close the door again.

"Must be some freak of nature," Levi assured them, "It'll probably be gone by afternoon." He was wrong.

It was three days before the storm was over. They shoveled their way out to a strange sight. The road was obliterated and only the tops of houses could be seen. It took Levi all day to make his way into town and he came back badly shaken. He had learned the snow usually lasted until spring.

CHAPTER EIGHTEEN

Christmas was dismal. The only presents, warm mittens and scarves, from the LaBlancs, were more than welcome. Jenny's mother had sent her a heavy woolen shawl which she wore continuously.

When the road to town was cleared, the children were finally able to go to school. Levi went to town often and began staying longer each time. He had learned that most of the locals gathered at the general store daily. Any news from the surrounding area was discussed there.

The long winter wore on. The children were sick with colds most of the time and had runny noses. The smell of camphor permeated the shabby house. Jenny herself, developed a bad cough.

"Let's go out and make a snow fort," Carl suggested one afternoon after a fresh snow had prevented the children from going to school.

Victor and Clayton and Blanche agreed and began to pull on their coats.

"Don't want to go out," Abner argued, "It's too cold."

"You're too little anyway," Carl turned away from him with a knowing smile.

"Am not!" Abner argued, "Just don't want to."

"Good! You stay inside with the babies," Carl said pulling on his hat and mittens.

Abner looked at his younger brother playing on the floor near his mother who sat in a rocker by the stove rocking the youngest. He quickly grabbed his coat and followed the others out into the snow.

The sharp blast of cold air from the open door started Jenny coughing.

"You should see a doctor." Beatrice said looking at her mother. A worried frown crossed her features.

"Nonsense, just hand me the onion syrup. It'll fix me right up." Jenny assured her.

Beatrice took down the brown bottle from the shelf and handed it to her mother.

"Could you pour me a spoonful, dear? I don't want to disturb the baby." Jenny asked. Beatrice poured the thick, smelly, medicine out for her mother and watched as she sipped it.

"Thank you, Bea. I'll be fine now." she said closing her eyes as she gently rocked the baby.

Beatrice stared out the window. How she hated this place! If only they had let her go stay with Aunt Marie. She glanced over at her mother's flushed face. What would they do if Mamma got really sick. She didn't want to think about it.

Jenny, not asleep, and aware of her daughter's scrutiny also wondered what would become of her family if she got too ill to care for them. She just couldn't let that happen! It was just a cold and she would be better soon she assured herself.

Levi finally returned from town and the children followed him into the house, eager for any news he might have to share, but their father was in a dark mood and had nothing to say. They quietly hung their coats on pegs by the stove and put their boots behind to dry.

Jenny soon had supper on the table. Levi said grace and the children eagerly dove into the bowls of boiled potatoes and turnips. They spread lard on thick slices of bread and washed it down with weak tea.

When the table was cleared and dishes put away Levi read a short passage from the bible. When he was done they all knew it was time for bed and they quickly settled in for the night.

Levi banked the coals in the cook stove which was also used for heat, and blew out the lamp. It had been quiet for about an hour when Jenny woke. "Levi!" she said shaking her husband. "I smell smoke." Roused, he fumbled for a match to light the lamp. As he rose to investigate his nostrils filled with an acrid smell of burning leather.

As he Reached the stove he opened the oven door and pulled out a pair of charred boots. "Who's are these?" he roared.

"Mine, Papa," Abner's voice piped up, "I wanted them to dry good so I put them inside."

Without a word, Levi strode across the room to the door and flung the charred boots out in the snow. "You better not expect a new pair," he grumbled as he made his way back to bed.

True to his word, though the cold, freezing winter Levi would not purchase another pair of boots for the boy.

Abner became resourceful. When he couldn't borrow a pair from one of his brothers he wrapped heavy paper over two pairs of socks and tied it with twine. His feet were often pink with cold but he had learned his lesson.

On an especially bleak day early in March, Beatrice was again complaining. "Why did we ever leave Michigan? It's never going to warm up."

Her parents ignored her but Carl had enough, "If you don't stop your bellyaching I'm goin' to throw you out in the snow 'til it melts."

"I'd like to see you try it," Beatrice stared at her younger brother fists clenched.

"Stop it! Both of you!" Jenny rose to stand between the children and a fit of coughing racked her.

"Sit down Mamma," Carl urged, quickly sorry for upsetting his mother. Levi stared at his wife. The winter had taken it's toll on all of them but Jenny looked bad. Her thin face was drawn and pale.. Brown eyes that had always sparkled, looked dull and tired. He would have to find something for his family soon.

When the thaw finally came Levi headed for town determined to find a farm to buy. Day after day he returned with no news.

Jenny was attempting to plant a small garden in the soil that was still cold when she looked up and saw Levi coming down the road. It was only midday and at first she hoped he was coming home early with good news, but as he drew near she noted the way he was dragging his feet. It had to be more bad news. She pulled her shawl around her and waited.

Levi came into the yard and stood before his wife. Silently he pulled a folded telegram from his pocket. "What is it?" she asked staring into his face. "Levi tell me!" He thrust the paper into her hands. Her eyes filled with tears as she tried to read. George LaBlanc was dead. He had fallen off a ladder and broke his neck. Her Papa was gone! Jenny's knees gave way and Levi caught her. He held his wife in silence as sobs shook her small frame.

Jenny pulled back and dried her eyes. "Poor Mamman," she choked back a sob, "How will she ever manage alone?"

Levi looked into his wife's troubled eyes and patted her arm, clumsily. "Maybe we should go back."

"Oh, Levi. Do you mean it?" Jenny searched his face. "I know how much you wanted to come here."

"Seems like I was wrong." He said gruffly. Turning, he headed for the door. "Write your Ma and tell her we'll be comin' home. I'll see to things."

If he heard the hoot of joy from Beatrice as he went out, he didn't let on.

Jenny watched her husband going down the path. His shoulders slumped like a beaten man. She hated seeing him like this but the thought of going home to Michigan was like a great weight had lifted from her. Within a week they had packed up their meager belongings, sold the cow and chickens and were on a train heading back to Michigan.

CHAPTER NINETEEN

Beatrice stood by the corner of the barn pulling on the worn rope attached to the dinner bell. As she yanked, a furry object landed at her feet. Looking up, she saw a red thatch of curls poking out of the hayloft door. "Abner?" she shouted, "What are you doing up there?"

"I'm showing Clayton how kittens can fly," came the reply. Just then another grey ball of fur came hurtling down, its legs outstretched. It hit the ground in a cloud of dust. The tiny cat shook itself and limped away under the fence.

"you do that again and I'll come up there and see if you can fly," Beatrice threatened. The two heads disappeared amid giggles. She gave one more lusty yank to the bell an turned toward the house. A warm breeze tangled her thick auburn hair. She absently brushed it back from her face surveying the scene before her.

The drab house listed slightly and the front porch sagged from the weight of many years of Michigan snows. New shingles stood out in patches on the roof where her father and brothers had tried to repair the many leaks. The old Patoux farm belonged to the Wakefords now. They hadn't had much choice when the returned from Idaho. Aunt Dehlia and Uncle Marcel had wasted no time moving in with Grandma LaBlanc. Their run-down farm was the only place in the area for sale. Reluctantly, Levi bought it from his brother-in-law and moved in with his family.

Beatrice turned away from the dismal view of bare fields and broken fences. She hadn't thought anything could be as bad as Idaho, until now. At least, when they lived there it always had been a hope that Papa would find a better place. Now, all she could see ahead was years of staying on this god-forsaken farm.

The boys darted past pulling her apron strings. "You brats! Just wait 'til I catch you." She shook her fist. Brothers! She was so sick of them. It was bad enough she had to wash their clothes, wipe their noses and empty their slop jars but putting up with teasing was something she didn't have to abide and she would get revenge. She strode purposefully toward the house.

She opened the door and was greeted with, "Beatrice, look to the bread. I think it's burning." She ran to the stove and with her apron wrapped around her hand, pulled out four smoking loaves. She sat them on the table fanning them while the smoke rose toward the ceiling.

"Where's Blanche?" she asked, turning towards her mother who sat in the corner nursing the newborn, Earl. "She took the bucket to the pump a while ago," Jenny sighed, "Don't know what's keeping her."

"You make sure you tell Pa it was her fault!" Beatrice muttered, "She was supposed to be watching."

Levi and Carl approached the house and through the window she heard the voice of Blanche, "Look at the pretty flowers I picked for Ma." Beatrice's mouth clamped shut as she vowed punishment on her sister.

She sullenly turned to the task of setting the table. Bringing heaping bowls of beans and salt pork she set them before her father and brothers. Blanche took Bernadette on her lap and buttered a slice of singed bread for the little girl.

"Aren't you coming to the table, Mama?" Carl asked, looking over at his mother still rocking the baby.

"I'll eat later," she said, smiling at her son. "I would like a cup of tea, though."

The girl had just sat down at her place and filled her plate when she heard her father's gruff voice. "Beatrice, fetch your Ma some tea."

"Be careful you don't spill it." Abner whispered.

She rose with a sigh. As she filled a steaming mug, she noted her mother's pale face. she fervently wished she would get better.

Mamma had never been herself since their trip to Idaho. As a consequence, more of the chores had fallen on Beatrice. When she returned to the table the salt pork was missing from her plate. She eyed her brothers who where mopping up the last of the beans with their bread with suspicion.

"The fields are waiting," Levi announced, pushing his chair back, "Come on Carl. Abner, you better come along too." The two boys jumped up to follow their father out the door. Abner, excited that his father had included him, rushed around the end of the table just as Beatrice's foot shot out. He pitched face down on the rough wooden floor. His outraged sobs rang through the kitchen. Beatrice, hid her smile.

"Maybe you better stay behind," Levi called back over his shoulder as he went out the door, "He'd probably fall under one of the horses." He was heard to mutter.

"She tripped me!" fell on deaf ears and he ran to his mother.

"There, there," Jenny soothed, wiping his tears, "You can go next time." He blew his nose noisily in her handkerchief. "Why don't you and Clayton go out to the barn and look for eggs."

"He'll probably break them all," Beatrice sniffed as she cleared the plates from the table.

"Will not!" he gave his sister a glower and ran out the door. Beatrice washed the dishes in silence ignoring Blanche who cheerfully hummed while she dried and put them away. Their next task was cleaning the globes of the kerosene lamps. Her mind was far away from her task. She thought, as she often did, of her Aunt Marie's house with the shiny electric lights that never got dirty and the clean water that came from a spigot. One day, she meant to have a house like that. She would have wallpaper with big red roses and—. She was startled from her reverie by her mother's coughing spell.

"Mamma?" she turned to see her mother in a coughing spasm, trying to steady herself as she lay Earl in his cradle. Beatrice ran to her side. As she put her arm around her mother's shoulders she felt how thin the woman had become.

"You should go see Doctor Billot," Beatrice scolded as she eased her mother into the rocker.

"Just give me my cough medicine," Jenny motioned to the cupboard, "I'll be fine."

Beatrice poured out a spoonful of the dark liquid made from onions and watched as her mother swallowed.

"Amy Farnsworth's mother was sick and Doctor Billot fixed her right up."

"If Mrs. Farnsworth wants to spend her husband's money on foolishness that's her business but all I need is your grandma's cough medicine to make me well." Jenny rose from her chair. Steadying herself, she smiled weakly at her daughter. "You've been spending a lot of time at the Farnsworths lately."

"Amy's my best friend."

"Amy's brother, Jed has a crush on her." Blanche piped up. "He wants her to go to the corn roast."

"I'm not sure Papa would approve of that," Jenny said, looking closely at her daughter's flushed face. Memories of long ago came flooding back. How many years had it been since Marie and Dehlia had teased her about Levi? It was hard to believe her daughter old enough for a beau but at fifteen there was no denying she was a beauty and boys were sure to notice.

"Do you really want to go with Jed?"

"I don't know yet." Beatrice lifted her chin defiantly.

"Your father never had much use for the Farnsworths." Jenny said. "But if you really want to go, I'll speak to him."

"*If* I decided to go with Jed," Beatrice said hotly, "I'll tell Papa myself."

Jenny looked at her willful daughter and sighed. There would be yet another confrontation between them. There wasn't much she could do. It had always been this way.

CHAPTER TWENTY

"Now Jed, you wouldn't want me to call my Pa," Beatrice pressed her hands against the boy's chest, coyly turning her head.

"You wouldn't do that," he said nuzzling her neck.

They stood in the shadow of the Wakeford barn. He was right. She wouldn't call her father. If he knew she was secretly meeting Jed he would—she didn't even want to think about it. Instead, she lifted her lips to his. Eagerly returning his kisses.

He was the first boy she had ever let close to her. She wasn't sure if it was his straw colored hair and blue eyes that won her or the fact that her father didn't like him or his father. A little of both maybe, but she found the power she had over this eager boy more exhilarating than anything she had ever experienced.

"I've got to go," she said at last, drawing away.

"Not yet," he whispered, holding her closer. His lips seeking hers.

"No, I mean it, Jed. They'll send someone looking for me."

With one last lingering kiss, the boy let her go with a promise to meet him the next night.

"Bea, where are you?" Blanche's voice came in the darkness. Beatrice brushed back her hair and came around the corner of the barn to see her sister coming down the path from the outhouse.

"I'm right here. What do you want?"

"Who was that you were talking to?" Blanche asked accusingly.

"You're hearing things," Beatrice said, brushing past her, "I was just getting some fresh air."

"You better not be meeting that Jed Farnsworth or Papa will skin you both!"

"Mind your own business," she said as she strode purposefully toward the house.

Lying in her bed that night Beatrice couldn't sleep. On the pretext of visiting her friend Amy, she had been meeting her brother Jed for six months. At twenty, he swore his undying love and begged her to marry him. While she used the excuse of fearing her father, she was sixteen now and knew there wasn't much Levi could do if she ran off with Jed. The real reason for hesitating was Beatrice knew she didn't quite return Jed's feelings. One of his promises, however, was a place of their own on his family's large farm and it was tempting. She tossed on her feather mattress thinking about Jed. He was so big and strong but he did have a temper. She remembered the time it got the best of him when he thought Henry Miller was giving her the eye. Poor Henry. She smiled to herself. It took two men to pull Jed off and seeing them fight over her had given her such a thrill. Good thing Jed hadn't realized she was the one doing the flirting.

One day soon, she would say yes and there would be no more taking care of her brothers and sisters.

The day came sooner than she had planned. It was a Sunday afternoon. Homer and Roy had come home for dinner. They were having a game of horseshoes with their father and Carl. The younger children were playing tag in the yard. All looked up when a horse and buggy came up the road in a cloud of dust.

"What does he want?" Homer scowled, recognizing Jed Farnsworth. They had been boyhood enemies and he wasn't about to welcome him.

Undaunted, Jed got down from his rig and strode up to the porch. Beatrice peered out the window. Her heart raced as she noted Jed's Sunday clothes and his slicked back hair. *What was he doing here?*

"Afternoon, Mr. Farnsworth," Jenny spoke politely through the screen door. "Mr. Wakeford's out back."

"Is Beatrice home," Jed stood twisting his hat, trying to peer past into the house.

"What do you want with her?" Jenny asked, arms folded, blocking the door.

"It's alright, Mama," Beatrice brushed past her. She searched Jed's face for an explanation. Surely he hadn't had the nerve to come calling on her when her brothers were home.

"It's Amy, she fell and hurt herself. She keeps asking for you." He blurted.

"Can I go, Mamma?" Beatrice turned to her mother, "Amy's my best friend."

"Well, I don't know." Jenny paused, looking at her husband.

"What's your business here, Farnsworth?" Levi asked, rounding the corner of the house.

"It's his sister, Amy," Beatrice explained, running down the steps to stand between him and Jed. "She's hurt and she sent Jed to fetch me."

"Hurt how?" Levi narrowed his eyes.

"She fell off her horse and hit her head," Jed replied, "Her leg is real bad."

"Oh, Pa" Beatrice pleaded, "Let me go see my friend."

"I suppose you can go," Levi reluctantly agreed, "But mind, you bring my girl home before dark."

Jed assured him he would bring her home early and helped Beatrice up into the buggy.

"How is Amy? Is she hurt bad?" She asked as they left the Wakeford farm in a flurry.

"Not so's you'd notice," Jed turned to smile at her. "She's waiting at the church with the preacher."

"What are you talking about?" Beatrice stared at him incredulously. "What preacher?"

Jed pulled the horse to a halt and turned to take her hands in his. "Bea, you knowed how much I love you and been wantin' to marry you." She nodded her eyes wide.

"Preacher, Norman is here today." he hurriedly went on. "If we get married this afternoon, your Pa can't stop us."

Beatrice heart was racing. Should she marry this boy against her father's wishes? He never liked the Farnsworths, claimed they were liars. Something had happened a long time ago between their fathers. What did it matter now?

"He'll have a fit!" she argued, but tantalizing thoughts filled her head. No more being told what to do. A place of her own. She looked at Jed and saw all her dreams coming true. Putting all thoughts of her parent's displeasure behind her she raised her chin.

"We'd best hurry." she said, smiling at her soon to be husband.

It was past sundown when Levi rode into the Farnsworth farmyard.

Lights flickered in the parlor windows as he strode up onto the porch. He rapped sharply on the door. It was opened by Mrs. Farnsworth, a tall thin woman with deep lines etched around her mouth.

"Sorry to hear about your daughter," he mumbled, "I've come to take Beatrice home, now."

"You'd best ask her about that," the woman smiled a knowing smile. Peering over her shoulder he could see Amy standing next to Beatrice. The girl seemed to have recovered. His eyes narrowed as he looked closer and saw her brother, Jed, standing next to Beatrice with his arm around his daughter's shoulder possessively.

"What's goin' on here?" he roared, pushing his way inside the door .

"Hold on there, Wakeford!" Mr. Farnsworth stepped in front of him blocking his path. He was a head shorter than Levi but solidly built.

"It come as a surprise to us, too, but there's no call to upset the children on their wedding day."

"What nonsense are you talking about?" Levi stared at his daughter in disbelief, "Get yourself out to the rig, girl!"

"She's not going with you," Jed stepped forward, "She's staying here with me, her husband." "Beatrice? What's he talkin' about?" Levi stared at the couple.

"There's nothin you can do, Papa," She stared defiantly at him, "We were married today by Preacher, Norman."

They all watched warily, as Levi's eyes turned into pinpoints. He began to shake with rage. His big hands curled in lethal fists as he charged the boy.

"Papa! Don't!" Beatrice screamed, throwing herself in front of Jed. Levi couldn't stop a smashing blow that caught the girl on the temple. She dropped to the floor like a stone.

He stood blinking at the still form of his daughter unaware of the commotion around him. Jed knelt down and gently cradled her in his arms. Picking her up, he carried his wife to the horsehair sofa. Amy was crying and her mother was screaming at her husband to get Levi out of the house.

It wasn't until Beatrice's eyes fluttered open and she tried to sit up, that things quieted. Looking around the room, she took a deep breath as her gaze fell on her father standing, trancelike, his arms hanging loose at his sides.

"Papa?" She rose unsteadily. She shook off Jed's arm as he tried to hold her back. She'd seen her father like this before and knew he wouldn't hurt anyone now.

"I'm sorry, we didn't tell you." She stood before him, looking up into his face.

His eyes began to focus and the pain in them almost brought tears to hers.

"I'm not coming with you, Pa." she said softly.

Levi took one last look at his daughter, turned on his heel and walked out the door.

CHAPTER TWENTY-ONE

Jenny picked up her last parcel and carried it to the wagon. Levi wouldn't like it, but she was going to see Beatrice. She had waited for almost a month thinking the girl would come home for her things but as each day passed she grew more worried. What if Levi had misunderstood and it was all a terrible mistake. She had to see her daughter and find out for herself.

She had waited until Levi and the boys were mending fences in the north fields and then loaded the wagon with some of Beatrice's clothes and her favorite quilt.

The Farnsworth farm was not far and Jenny soon pulled into the yard. She had to admit the house was grand. It was a large two storied affair with a fancy porch across the front. Seeing a flutter of curtains in the front window she climbed down and crossed the well- kept barn yard. She took a deep breath and knocked on the door. It was opened by Mrs. Farnsworth who stood silently staring. Was that a smug smile? It was hard to tell from her lips set in a tight line. Jenny looked down, aware of her faded blue gingham dress and worn bonnet. "I'm here to see my daughter, Fiona." she said, raising her chin purposefully, refusing to be intimidated by the woman in the dark silk dress. Stepping back, the woman reluctantly opened the door and motioned Jenny to come in.

It took a minute for Jenny's eyes to adjust to the cool dark parlor. Heavy lace curtains covered the windows keeping out the morning rays of the sun. she jumped when the chimes of a tall grandfather's clock rang out. Looking up the polished stairway, she saw her daughter on the stairs.

"Mama, what are you doing here?" she asked, as she slowly descended.

"I—I came to bring you your things." Jenny stared at her daughter. Beatrice paused for a moment and then ran down the stairs to embrace her mother.

"I thought you'd never want to see me again," Beatrice gulped through her tears.

"How could you think that?" Jenny patted her gently.

"Jed told me you all hated me for running off like we did." She looking hopefully at her mother, "But you don't, do you?"

"I'll have to admit, you took us by surprise," Jenny admitted, "But if you're happy, I doesn't matter."

"What about Papa?" Beatrice asked, searching her mother's face.

"Well, he's still a might put out with Jed sneakin' you off like he did," Jenny admitted, "But you know Papa loves you and he'll come around."

"Please sit down, Mamma," Beatrice urged her toward the horsehair sofa.

"I can't stay too long," Jenny said as she sat gingerly on the hard seat, "I just wanted to bring you some of your things."

Jenny turned to look closely at her daughter who moved nervously from the sofa to the mantel, picking up a silver frame and putting it down. "What is it, Beatrice?" her mother asked, quietly, "Aren't you happy?"

"Of course I'm happy," the girl protested, "I've got a fine husband."

"How long are you going to live here with his folks?" her mother asked, pointedly. The girl might not want to admit it, but something was definitely wrong.

"Jed promised he'd build us a place as soon as planting season is over," Beatrice assured her.

From long experience with the willful girl Jenny knew there was no point in pressing the issue. "I've got to be going," She said, rising. "Come out to the wagon and get your belongings."

"Why don't you give my clothes to Blanche," Beatrice said looking over the pitiful bundle her mother had brought, "Jed took me to town and got me all new things."

"What about the quilt Grandma made for you?" Jenny said, trying to hide the hurt of her daughter's scorn.

"I guess I could use it," Beatrice reluctantly picked up the dark patchwork bundle, thanks."

"I'd better be getting along." Jenny said, climbing up into the wagon. "If you should need—" Jenny's voice trailed off.

"Don't worry. I'm fine." Beatrice's chin rose. "Thanks for coming, Ma."

Jenny nodded to her daughter, snapped the reins, and headed out of the yard.

Beatrice stood clutching her grandmother's blanket and watched until her mother disappeared from view around the bend that lead from the Farnsworth farm.

She buried her face in the soft familiar smell of the quilt blinking back tears. If her mother had only known how much she wanted to go with her.

"Beatrice?" Mrs. Farnsworth's high pitched voice, called from the house, "Come help me with the vittles."

"Coming," she sighed and turned toward the house. She didn't know which was worse, her mother-in-law's nagging or his father's knowing looks and constant remarks about when could he expect a grandson.

Her friend Amy wasn't much help either. She was conveniently absent when it came time to empty slop jars or scrub floors. All the hard work fell on her. It was almost like being home with her sister Blanche.

Not quite, though. Even though she had been raised on a farm and Lord knows, she had heard enough sounds from her parents rooms over the years to know what marriage meant, she was not prepared for her wedding night. Jed's demanding lust for her was not only painful, but once satisfied, he fell asleep. She tried to slide away from his tight embrace but he only grunted and began snoring in her ear. She gritted her teeth and tried to fight the panic that rose in her. How could she endure years of this? She lay staring into the dark trying to fight the overwhelming fear of being trapped.

"You went to see her, didn't you?" Levi's voice came out of the darkness. Jenny laying next to her husband had thought him asleep.

"Yes, I did." She admitted.

"She all right?"

"Says she is," Jenny hesitated, "New clothes and all, but I think her willfulness might have gotten her into somethin' she wasn't ready for."

"Those Farnsworth's are a lying bunch." Levi's voice trembled, "Hard tellin' what was promised her to talk her into marryin' that boy of theirs."

"She's so young—" Jenny tried to hold back a sob.

"Don't fret," Levi's big hand reached for Jennys. "Those Farnsworths don't know Beatrice like we do. They might have got a little more than they bargained for."

CHAPTER TWENTY-TWO

How much more could she take? Beatrice snapped the reins of the horse impatiently. In spite of all his promises to build them a place of their own, she and Jed still lived with his parents. His mother was a stern task master with a list of chores from morning until she climbed the stairs for bed at night.

Bed! what a nightmare it had become. Jed wanting to please his father, insisted they try every night to produce an heir to the Farnsworth name. She tried everything she could to dissuade him, from tears to pretending sleep but nothing worked. The more she protested the more eager he became, to the point of violence at times. She reached up to adjust the scarf around her neck. She didn't want to explain the bruise she had acquired last night. Much to her relief, however, she had not yet become pregnant. Knowing it was probably just a matter of time, the thought still terrified her.

Beatrice urged the horse faster. She was on her way to see her new baby sister. How did Mama do it? She welcomed child after child with so much love. She pulled into the yard and hitched the horse by the water trough. She watched as her sisters ran down the steps to meet her. Blanche, almost as tall as she was now with Bernadette toddling after her.

"What a pretty hat!" Blanche said, reaching up to touch the smart feather. "What are your shoes made of?"

"They call it suede," Beatrice told her, basking in the envy of her younger sister. At least, Jed had kept one promise. She did have nice clothes.

She stood looking at the run down farm with mixed thoughts. The Farnsworth's, where she now lived, was much finer with it's huge house and neat farm buildings but it was a cold silent place. Beatrice turned to hear her little brothers, Victor and Clayton as they came running from the barn shouting greetings to her. Strange, she'd never thought she would miss the sound of children's laughter but for a moment she actually felt homesick. Quickly, shaking it off, she followed her sisters into the house.

"Come see your new sister?" Mama smiled at her from the rocker by the stove.

Beatrice bent to kiss her mother and was startled by the tiny perfect face peeking out at her from a worn blanket.

Her other siblings had all looked pretty much the same, with red faces and little hair but this child was like one of the little china cherubs her mother-in-law had setting on the mantel. The baby's skin was a delicate shade of pink. Soft yellow fuzz covered her head and the most startling blue eyes peered out from under golden eyelashes. It was as if the baby could actually see her.

"She's beautiful, Mama," Beatrice said reaching down to touch the little hand that escaped the blanket. Tiny fingers curled around hers with surprising strength. "What did you name her?"

"This is your new sister, Emma." Jenny smiled proudly up at her daughter, "Would you like to hold her?"

Beatrice hesitated, puzzled by her feelings for this perfect child. Gingerly, she lifted the infant from her mother's outstretched arms. The baby's eyes never left her face.

"She's such a joy," Jenny smiled, "I've never even heard her cry, except when Papa helped me bring her into the world and that was just a little squeak."

"Papa delivered her?" Beatrice asked, in disbelief. "Where was Grandma?"

"Emma came so fast, we didn't have time to fetch her." *Emma, what a plain name.* Beatrice thought to herself, *If she were mine I'd name her Antoinette or Juanita.*

"Are you thinking about having one of your own," Her mother's voice brought her back to reality.

Beatrice stared at her mother, "No! not yet." Turning, she thrust the baby back into her mother's arms. "I can't stay long. Just wanted to bring you this." She reached for a package wrapped in shiny white paper she had left on the table.

"Blanche, open it for Mamma" Beatrice urged. Her sister eagerly obeyed and held up a tiny pink crocheted sweater and bonnet to match.

"It's lovely," Jenny said, awed by the delicate softness. "Did you make it?"

"You know I'm no good at such things," Beatrice admitted, "I bought it in Cheyboygan. Here, try it on her." The soft pink bonnet brought out the delicate rose in the baby's cheeks making her more adorable than before.

"Never had any store bought things for the other children," Jenny sighed, looking down at her newest daughter. "Don't know if Papa will approve of such finery."

"Is it because it came from me?" Beatrice frowned.

"Of course not," her mother assured her, "You know what a proud man your father is."

Beatrice knew how proud her father was, all right. Angry thoughts came flooding back. She remembered when he had come to Detroit to fetch her home from her Aunt Marie's and what a fuss he had made over her new clothes.

"You could tell him Grandma made the sweater," She suggested.

"I would never lie to your father," Jenny frowned at her daughter. "Besides, he knows how crippled Grandma's hands are."

"She's such a beautiful baby," Beatrice reached down and touched the infants downy cheek. "She deserves to have something special."

"Don't fret," Jenny assured her, "It'll be all right."

"I can't stay," Beatrice looked nervously out the window. She wasn't ready for a confrontation with her father today. With a sigh, she hugged her mother and turned to go.

All the way back to the Farnsworth's Beatrice tried to put the picture of her new little sister out of her mind. She saw her growing up wearing Bernadette's hand- me-downs, never knowing what a new pair of shoes felt like. She didn't know how she would do it, but this perfect little girl deserved better and she would somehow see that she got it.

CHAPTER TWENTY-THREE

It was early in the morning when the train heading south from Cheyboygan puffed into the Wolverine station. Drops of rain hissed as they fell on the steaming engine. No one noticed the dark figure that darted from the side of the station and slipped up into the passenger car. She sat huddled in the far corner seat of the car clutching a small bag.

Taking a quick glance out of the window, Beatrice breathed a sigh of relief as the train began moving. Hopefully, he wouldn't miss her until his father called him for morning chores.

She sat back in the seat and the last twenty-four hours played over in her head.

Jed and his Pa had been to town playing cards and drinking, as usual. He'd come stumbling up the stairs to their room. She turned to the wall feigning sleep.

"Wake up! Your lovin' husband's home," He called in a hoarse whisper. When she didn't respond, he jerked her quilt away, reached over, and brought his big hand down on her bottom with a playful slap. "Leave me alone," Beatrice muttered, sliding away from him on the other side of the bed.

Undaunted, Jed grabbed her ankle and pulled her across the bed fighting and kicking. She tried to fend him off but his big hands held her wrists.

Looking into his reddened face and small mean eyes she wondered how she had ever thought him handsome.

He'd come home drunk many times and the result had always been the same. He seemed to take pleasure in overpowering her. This time, however, the sickening smell of his whiskey breath enraged her. If he had seen the look in her eyes he may have hesitated but instead he tore at her nightgown. Struggling, she managed to free her right hand. Reaching out, her fingers closed around the china pitcher on the bedside table. With all her strength, she brought it down on Jed's head. He gave a small shudder and went limp.

It wan't easy, but she managed to slide out from under his body and stood looking down at his still form. Relieved to see him breathing, but terrified of what would happen when he woke up, she knew what she must do. She dressed quickly.

Beatrice listened at the door and was met with silence. Hopefully, her in-laws were asleep. She turned back to the bed. Carefully, she slid her hand in her husband's pocket and grasped the money she found there. She quietly led the old mare out of the barn and climbed up on her back. The horse, disturbed from its rest, slowly plodded down the road. It was almost dawn when they approached Wolverine. Beatrice slid from the animal and gave it a smack on the rump, knowing it would find it's way back home.

When the train pulled in, she hid in the shadows of the train depot until it was ready to leave. She didn't want to go into the station and take a chance of being seen buying a ticket. She was quite sure she could get one from the conductor. Looking both ways and seeing no one, she climbed aboard just as it pulled out.

"You're ticket, ma'am"

Beatrice looked up into the ruddy face of the conductor.

"I'd like to purchase one," she told him clutching her bag.

"How far are you going?"

"How much is a ticket to Detroit?"

"That'll be Thirteen dollars." The conductor eyed her suspiciously.

Beatrice reached into her bag and pulled out the crumpled money she had taken from Jed's pocket. She carefully counted out the bills and found to her disappointment, there was only eleven dollars. "How far will this take me?" She asked, thrusting the money at the conductor.

"Ten dollars and fifty cents will get you to Pontiac," the man told her.

"Fine," Beatrice sat up, straightening her hat, "That's where I want to go." Lifting her chin, she stared him down. The conductor shrugged and punched a ticket for her.

Sitting back in the seat clutching the fifty-cents change the man had given her, Beatrice fought back tears of frustration and a gnawing panic. She had planned to go to her Aunt Marie's in Detroit, certain that she would understand and help her. Now she was going to a town she'd never heard of. She closed her eyes and pictured Jed's face when he realized she was gone. He would be furious! Maybe it was a stroke of luck that she was going to this town of Pontiac. He would never think to look for her there. With a sigh, she leaned back against the plush seat and soon the rhythm of the train carrying her through the early morning light lulled her to sleep.

It was almost dark when the train pulled into the Pontiac Station. Beatrice peered anxiously out the window. A lantern hung by the platform, cast eerie shadows. She stepped down from the car and looked around. Squaring her shoulders, she started down a worn path that led toward the winking lights of town. Soon she came to tree lined thoroughfare. There seemed to be several small shops on the other side. She crossed over the quiet street. Most of the stores were closed but a warm glow shining from the windows of a small cafe drew her in. Upon entering, she realized she hadn't eaten all day and the delicious smell of hot biscuits nearly overwhelmed her.

"You all right, Miss?" A plump, rosy cheeked woman approached her with concern on her face.

"I'm fine," Beatrice said, steadying herself.

"Sit right here," the woman said, showing her to a small table with a checkered tablecloth. "Would you like a cup of tea?"

"Yes, thank you." Beatrice's stomach was growling. She felt around in the bottom of her bag and her fingers closed on the fifty cent piece the conductor had given her. She studied the menu written on a slate board above the counter and ordered the blue plate special for fifteen cents.

The friendly proprietor brought her a heaping plate of beef stew with steaming biscuits which she made short work of. Feeling somewhat better, Beatrice sat sipping her tea. Wondering what she was going to do. Having no money, she had decided on the train to sell her jewelry. A locket and cameo brooch Jed had given her should bring enough to see her through until she could contact her Aunt Marie, but what about tonight? She had no where to go.

"Would you like more tea?" the friendly waitress asked. Beatrice nodded absently.

"Pardon me Miss, but you look so troubled," the woman said, filling her cup from a china teapot. "Is there something I can do to help you? My name's Lucy and that's my husband, Sam." She pointed toward the back where a stoop shouldered man was wiping the counter trying not to stare. "What's your name, dear?"

"Bea, Bea Worth" Beatrice found herself lying. It had come easily since she had been around the Farnsworths. "I don't know what to do. My aunt Marie was supposed to meet my train. I haven't a place to stay." she looked woefully at the woman, her eyes filling with tears.

"There's a small room with a cot behind the kitchen where Sam takes a nap. It's not much but you can stay there if you'd like." the woman offered. "We live upstairs."

"Oh, I couldn't impose like that," Beatrice protested weakly, dabbing at her eyes with a napkin.

"Now, now, you just come along with me," the woman insisted, "It's not right for a lady, like yourself to be out alone after dark."

"Thank you Lucy, you're so kind." Beatrice said gratefully following the woman through the kitchen through a curtain to a small storage room. A wooden cot sat between some crates against the wall. Gingerly, she sat down and looked around. It would have to do. Anything was surely better than sleeping in the train station.

"Levi! come quick!" Jenny had just finished feeding the chickens when she saw two horses coming up the road at a fast gallop.

Her husband strode out on the porch and peered at the two approaching riders. "Farnsworths," he said with distaste.

"What do you suppose they want?" Jenny said twisting her apron in her hands.

Levi stood silently watching as Jed and his father jumped down from panting horses.

"You tell Beatrice to come on out or I'll come in and get her!" Jed demanded as he strode toward the house.

"If you're looking for your wife, she's not here," Levi answered him coldly. "And, neither you or your Pa are comin' into my house."

"I know your hidin' her," Jed snarled, but hesitated. The look in Levi's cold blue eyes held him from coming any closer.

"Why do you think she's here?" Jenny asked.

"She's run off, that's why." The elder Farnsworth stood next to his son.

"What did you do to her?" Jenny asked accusingly.

"Never mind that. Look what she done to Jed." His father said pointing to the bandage on his son's head. "Tried to kill the boy whilst he was sleeping." Levi stepped down from the porch and faced the two men, "The girl's not here and if I find out you done something to her, you'll answer to me."

The Farnsworth's looked at each other and backed away muttering.

"Where do you suppose she's gone?" Jenny said as she watched the Farnsworths ride away.

"Don't fret about Beatrice," Levi answered, a hint of a smile on his lips. "Did you see that bandage? The girl can take care of herself."

CHAPTER TWENTY-FOUR

Beatrice awoke to the tantalizing smell of coffee . Where was she? Then the enormity of what she had done came rushing back. She sat on the edge of the cot, her head in her hands. What in the world was she going to do? Jed would surely come looking for her. If he found her?—She didn't want to think about it. Looking around, she saw a basin sitting on a small table. With a sigh, she washed her face with cold water, swept back her unruly hair the best she could, and tried to smooth the wrinkles from her skirt.

She peered around the flowered curtain and saw Lucy, up to her elbows with flour, rolling out pies.

"Mornin' Have yourself a coffee," the woman motioned over her shoulder to the big pot that bubbled on the cook stove.

"Good morning," Beatrice answered, pouring herself a cup of steaming black liquid. "You were so kind to let me stay. Is there something I can do to help you?"

"Well, I am running a little late this morning," Lucy admitted. "If you could set napkins and spoons on the tables it would be a help." "I'll be glad to," Beatrice assured her.

"You'd better put on that apron by the door," Lucy motioned with a flour covered hand. "Wouldn't want you to get anything on your fine clothes. You'll find the napkins and such out front under the counter."

Beatrice followed her advice. Tying the apron, she found it nearly went around her twice, covering her from neck to ankle. Entering the cafe she saw several customers already sitting at the counter. Sam was flipping a stack of pancakes on the stove. He looked up, giving her a quizzical glance, shrugged his shoulders and turned back to his cooking.

She began setting up the tables. Before she was done, several customers had entered and were occupying them.

"Tell Sam I'll have my usual ham and eggs over easy," A short, stout man with white hair said, peering over his glasses. "You new here?"

"I—," Beatrice hesitated, not wanting to explain her presence.

"I'll have oatmeal and biscuits," another customer called out. She turned to see Sam motioning to her.

"They're regulars," he smiled at her. "I know what they want. If you'll just pour them coffee I'll have their orders right up." Before long, Beatrice found herself pouring coffee and setting plates before the customers with ease. After all, she had been serving meals to her family most of her life. The only difference being the customers treated her politely and smiled.

It was mid morning before the cafe had emptied.

Beatrice sat down at the counter and Lucy placed a fresh sugar doughnut and a cup of coffee before her.

"You were a mighty big help to me today, Bea" the woman said, wiping her hands on her apron. "We could sure use someone like you around here." she paused and her blue eyes searched Beatrice's. If you were stayin', I'd offer you a job."

"Well, I might be here for a while," Beatrice heard herself saying. "If I don't hear from my Aunt, that is."

"Can't pay much but Sam could fix up the store room for you and of course, your meals would be free."

"Guess I could stay on for a bit," Beatrice said slowly, not wanting to sound to eager.

"Good!, Lucy said, patting her arm. "I'll tell Sam."

Beatrice sat sipping her coffee trying not to smile. A big load had been lifted from her shoulders and it felt good to be appreciated for once. Maybe things were going to work out for her after all.

"What do you think?" Lucy nodded toward her new waitress pouring coffee.

"Seems to be a hard worker," Sam, her husband replied, as he stirred a pot of stew. "Business has sure picked up since she started."

"A pretty girl like that was bound to attract the fellas around here." Lucy admitted, "But, That's not what I meant. I'm wondering how long she will stay."

"Been here for some time now and ain't said nothing about leavin', has she?" Sam offered.

"No, she hasn't," Lucy mused, "But I can't help wonderin' why a nice girl like her would want to stay in our storeroom. I wonder why her Aunt never came for her.

"What are you frettin' about?" Sam frowned, "She's seems happy enough and the customers sure like her."

"Guess you're right," Lucy admitted. "At least she's got some color in her cheeks. When she first came she looked a might peaked."

"Been fillin' up on our good vittles." Sam remarked putting a lid on the simmering pot.

Across the room, Beatrice set a bowl of barley soup in front of a small man with wire rimmed glasses.

"Would you like more bread, Mr. Weiss?" she asked. Beatrice had learned the names of most of her customers and they all seemed to enjoy it. Herman Weiss owned a jewelry shop in the next block and was a regular.

"Yes, thank you Bea." the man smiled a wizened grin and helped himself to fresh bread from the basket she offered.

"Could I have more coffee, please?" A deep voice called to her from the corner table.

Beatrice turned to look at the big man sitting there with his long legs curled awkwardly under the table. "Coming right up, Doctor Morris." She called, noting his shy smile as she turned away. He was one of her regulars and always so polite.

"Did you see that?" Lucy nudged Sam, "Doc's on his fourth cup of coffee."

"He does seem to be comin' in regular since Bea's been here." Sam noted turning back to his cooking.

"Can't say I blame him." Lucy said peering around the corner at the couple. "She's such a pretty girl."

"Are you all right, Doctor Morris?" Bea looked down, noting the shadows under the man's gentle gray eyes as she filled his cup.

"Been up all night delivering the Tyler's new son," he said, spooning sugar into the strong black liquid.

"You should go home and get some rest," Bea said noting the tired slump of his big shoulders.

"Thanks for you're concern, Bea but I have to make a couple calls first," he said, draining his cup. With a sigh, he slowly pushed back his chair. He unfolded his long legs and stood towering above her. Beatrice stepped back nervously. He was much taller but his size brought back memories of Levi.

"Anything wrong?" The Doctor asked, looking at the frown that crossed her face.

"No, no," she assured him, "It's just that you remind me of someone."

"Someone you'd rather forget, I take it." His kindly eyes searched her face.

"It's my Pa," she admitted, "He's tall like you and we don't get along to well."

"Sorry to hear it." There was sincerity in his deep voice. "It must be hard for you, being away from your folks."

"Sometimes," she admitted, brushing away a tear that threatened to roll down her cheek.

"How would you like to come to dinner with me and my family?" he asked.

"That's very kind of you but I have to work." she said looking across the room at Lucy who was filling sugar bowls.

"I'm sure they could spare you one Sunday afternoon, couldn't you Lucy?" the doctor called to the woman.

"I guess we could manage," Lucy said, trying to hide a knowing look. "You can have next Sunday afternoon off, if you want."

"Good, then it's settled. I'll come for you at noon." the Doctor smiled down at Beatrice and turned to leave. "I'll tell my sister to expect company."

Sister! He didn't say wife. He said Sister. Beatrice didn't know why this made her feel so happy. She knew she had no right to be thinking of another man when she was married to Jed. Still, she'd never met a man as kind and thoughtful as Doctor Morris and she looked forward to dinner with him and his family.

"Bea, The Doc is here," Lucy called from the front of the cafe. The chimes from the courthouse clock were ringing out the noon hour.

Beatrice nervously smoothed a curl back under her hat and stepped out to meet him.

"You're looking very pretty today, Bea," the doctor smiled at her.

"Thank you," she replied, feeling her cheeks flush from his steady gaze.

"Shall we go?" he said, holding the door open.

"You run along now, Bea." Lucy called to her, "Have a nice time with the Doc's family."

"Thank you Lucy," Beatrice answered and turned to see the doctor offering her his arm.

"My Goodness!" Beatrice said, stopping outside the door. Her eyes grew wide with wonder at the shiny machine sitting at the curb.

"My old horse, Bob, gets me around to my patients out in the country but I'd rather try out my new Reo." He smiled his slow smile. "Unless you'd rather go in the buggy."

"I've never been in one of these—Autos before, Doctor Morris," Beatrice said, nervously eyeing the machine, "But I guess I could try it."

"Please call me John," he said. Bea felt the warmth from his strong hand on her arm as he helped her up onto the seat. He tucked a soft blanket around her and went to the front to turn the crank. After some sputtering, the engine caught and he climbed in beside her.

The machine slowly moved down Huron avenue. The Maples and Oaks lining the street where alive with fall colors of gold and red. At the court-house, they turned onto Saginaw street. Most of Pontiac's businesses lined the street. Bea caught glimpses of the shiny yellow car in the windows of the stores.

Once she got used to the noise, Beatrice tried to relax a little. They speeded up as they headed south out of town into the fall countryside.

"How do you like it?" he turned to smile at her.

Reluctant to admit the motion of the car was making her a bit queasy, she smiled, weakly and shouted above the noise, "It's very nice."

The Doctor, noting her flushed face as she made a grab for her hat and slowed down..

They chugged along in silence until they came to a sign announcing the town of Birmingham. It proved to be a very pretty place with giant Oaks lining the wide streets of large, two storied, homes. Soon, the doctor turned left into a circular driveway. He pulled hard on the hand brake and stopped before a stately brick house with white columns.

The double doors opened and a tall woman in a blue silk dress stood smiling as he helped Beatrice down.

"There's my sister Edith," the doctor said. He went up the steps and kissed the woman on the cheek. "Edith, this is Bea, the girl I was telling you about."

"So happy to meet you," His sister said, taking Beatrice's small hand in her own warm one. She ushered them into large hallway with shiny polished floors. A crystal chandelier sparkled in the sun coming from a cut glass window above the door.

"It's so nice of you to invite me," Beatrice said quietly, trying not to stare at her surroundings. She had thought her Aunt Marie's home to be grand but it couldn't compare to this one.

"It's about time you brought a lady to dinner." Edith admonished her brother, taking their coats and hanging them on a tall Oak halltree. She led them past a curved staircase. It rose from the right to a high balcony. "And, such a pretty one, too." John's sister said smiling, as she took Beatrice by the arm steering her into the parlor.

Heavy, cream colored drapes with fine sheer curtains hung from tall windows creating a soft light in the enormous room. Beatrice feet sunk into thick rich carpet. Looking down, she saw the pattern of large pink roses matched the flowers in the wallpaper. Stepping into the room she noted how the brocade sofas in shades of beige and rose were arranged cozily, flanked by polished tables holding graceful vases filled with Asters and mums. At first, Beatrice didn't see the man sitting before the fireplace in a velvet wing backed chair. He rose and came forward straightening his silk vest.

"John, good to see you," Said the man. He was almost as tall as the doctor and he strode across the room in a few steps to shake his hand heartily.

"Bea, this is Henri Armand, my brother-in-law," Doctor Morris said, introducing the man whose black eyes sparkled with interest.

Beatrice tried not to show how startled she was when Henri took her hand and brought it to his lips.

"Such a pleasure, my dear," He said, still holding her hand. "Why haven't you brought this lovely lady to meet us before, eh, John?"

"She is new to town," the doctor said smoothly. "Now have pity on her and let her sit down."

"So he brought you in his machine?" Henri chided, "How did you like his noisy toy?"

"It's a little windy but liked it very much," Beatrice said, recovering her composure.

"You are a brave young lady to ride with this wild young man," Henri chided, his eyes twinkling.

"Now, now, stop teasing," Edith said smiling at them from the doorway. A boy of about ten stood next to her.

"Uncle John!" he cried, running across the room to be lifted up by his uncle.

"Phillip, where are your manners?" his mother cautioned, "We have another guest."

Beatrice looked down at this little boy in velvet knickers with his dark hair smoothed back who politely held out his hand. With a pang, she thought of her brothers, Abner, Victor and the others whose hair never stayed combed. Suddenly, she missed them terribly.

Shortly, a maid in a starched white apron and cap appeared in the door and announced dinner was ready.

"I hope you don't mind if we eat in the small dining-room," Edith said ushering them into an alcove just off the parlor.

It didn't seem small to Beatrice. One wall of the room was french doors that led out to a stone porch and a view of a spacious yard . On the other side was a cherry sideboard covered with a linen scarf. The table was set with fine china and crystal goblets. In the center of the table was a large bowl of golden Chrysanthemums.

Beatrice found herself seated across the table from the doctor and his nephew. Edith sat at one end of the long table and Henri at the other.

First, the maid brought in a silver tureen from which she ladled hot pea soup into china bowls setting before them. It was followed by heaping platters of roast pork and lamb. Bowls of steaming mashed potatoes and golden squash were offered along with hot biscuits.

"Some more gravy, ma'am?" The maid offered.

Beatrice shook her head. She'd tried valiantly to nibble on the food but in truth, the pungent odors had left her stomach upset and fearful she would become ill, she ate very little.

"It's so good to have you home for dinner." Edith smiled at her brother. "He always tells me he is to busy." "Uncle John takes care of sick people, don't you?" Phillip said gazing up at his uncle.

Beatrice looked across the table and saw the doctor grinning down at his nephew. There was a definite family resemblance. Both had the same dark hair—.

She suddenly felt strange. Beatrice reached for a sip of water and to her horror watched as the goblet slowly dropped from her hand spilling it's contents on the white table linen. Then the room began to spin. The last thing she saw was the look of concern on the doctor's face as he jumped up and then everything went dark.

"She's waking up." Beatrice heard Edith's voice and slowly opened her eyes. Doctor Morris was holding a strong smelling vial under her nose.

"What happened?" she sputtered as she pushed his hand away. Trying to sit up, she looked around her and realized she was laying in large four poster bed.

"Don't try to get up yet," Doctor Morris said gently, "You fainted and I want to make sure you're all right." His grey eyes looked with concern into hers.

"I'm so sorry," Beatrice gulped. she felt her cheeks flush with embarrassment. "I don't know what happened."

"Don't worry about it," He said, taking her hand. We're just glad to see you come around." "I want you to rest for a while and then I'll take you back to Lucy's." The doctor smiled down at her.

"If you want anything, ring this. Edith held up a little silver bell on the night table."

She nodded meekly and watched as they all withdrew, leaving the door ajar.

"It was probably riding in that contraption of yours," she heard Henri's accusing voice as they descended the stairs. "The fumes would make anyone sick."

Beatrice lay staring at the ceiling. A nagging fear tugged at her. There had been other dizzy spells. She hadn't told Lucy, fearful she'd send her away. She had not had her monthly since she'd left home and she attributed it to her new strange surroundings. However, it could mean something else. What if she was carrying Jed's child? *I couldn't be true!* Not now, when she was at last free of him. Hot tears ran down her cheeks.

Sometime later, the doctor returned and sat on the edge of the bed. Noting her tear stained face, he tried to console her. "You musn't be so upset, Bea," he took her hand in his large one. "I'm the one who should have noticed the auto was making you sick. Can you ever forgive me?"

Beatrice looked into his handsome, caring face and words failed her.

"Edith wants you to spend the night," he said, "And I think it's a good idea."

"Oh no, I can't stay," Beatrice protested. "Lucy will worry."

"It will be all right. We'll let her know you're spending the night."

"But—I can't put your sister out." New tears began as the doctor brushed damp curls from her brow.

"I'm afraid I must insist." Edith said as she approached the bed with a steaming cup on a tray. "You are our guest and I can't let you leave until I know you're well." She held the cup to Beatrice's lips. "Please try to drink some. My brother has prescribed this for you and I'm sure it will make you feel better."

"The mild sedative in it should help." The Doctor smiled a reassuring smile as he rose, "Try to get some rest."

Beatrice, to weak to argue, drank the sweet tea and let Edith help her into a soft flannel nightgown. She sighed and lay back. She hadn't felt anything this soft since she had slept on her Grandma LaBlanc's feather mattress. She closed her eyes and heard Edith quietly leave the room.

What was she to do? She had written her Aunt Marie as soon as she had arrived in Pontiac and in her reply her aunt had advised Beatrice to stay where she was. Jed had already been to Detroit searching for her.

She knew her stay at Lucy's was temporary but everyone was so nice to her and it was the first time she could remember being so happy. Now this!

Her last thoughts, as the sedative took effect, were, 'I can't be pregnant. There must be some mistake.'

"Good morning!" Edith's cheerful voice came to Beatrice as she opened her eyes groggily and squinted at the sunlight streaming in from the window.

"How do you feel?" she asked approaching the bed with a wicker tray.

"Much better, thank you," Beatrice answered trying to rise.

"No, no, don't get up," Edith said placing the breakfast tray in front of her. "Wait until you've had some coffee and toast."

Beatrice dutifully sipped the hot liquid and tried to clear her head.

It all came back to her and she felt her cheeks flush with embarrassment. What must Dr. Morris, John, as he'd asked her to call him, and his sister think of her? They'd all been so kind and she'd wanted them to like her.

"There is a basin on the dresser if you want to freshen up," Edith smiled at her, "When you feel up to it, John is waiting downstairs."

Beatrice lay for a moment her fingers moving over the soft linen sheets, staring at the angels carved in the molding around the ceiling. What would it be like to live in a house like this?

With a sigh, she threw back the silk coverlet and rose. She was still a little light headed but shook it off and reached for her clothes.

CHAPTER TWENTY-FIVE

Beatrice said her good-byes and promised she would come back to dinner another time. She was a little disappointed to see the Doctor had brought his horse and buggy. She had to admit, however, much as she enjoyed the ride in his auto, the familiar swaying of the rig was much easier on her head, which still was a little fuzzy.

"Doctor Morris," Beatrice began.

"John, please call me John," he insisted.

"John," she began, "I'm sorry I embarrassed you. What must your family think of me?"

He placed his big hand over her small one. "You did not embarrass me, Bea. As for Edith and Henri, they really liked you and want you to come back."

"If you think they would have me, John," she hesitated, "I would very much like to see them again."

"Bea," he said slowing the horse to a walk, "I would like you to come to my office for a check up."

"But I'm fine," she replied trying to keep the panic from her voice.

"Just the same," he insisted, "I want to make sure you are all right." "I'll come to see you in a few days," she agreed, knowing she would delay the visit as long as she could

Lucy and Sam welcomed her and put her to work as soon as she got back. As she set plates before her customers she couldn't stop thinking about the tall handsome Doctor. She had never met anyone so gentle and kind.

On the way home, John had told her about his family. His father, had made his fortune in lumber, but died when he was quite young. Edith, who was four years older, had cared for their mother until she passed away a few years ago. When Edith and Henri got married they decided to stay on in the house where she had grown up. Returning from medical school, John decided he preferred a place of his own.

Knowing the doctor was wealthy made Beatrice think of him differently. She'd always felt a little sorry for him when he sat in the cafe drinking his black coffee, always making sure she gave him the largest donut. Now she wasn't sure how to behave.

The next few days she was unusually busy and Beatrice found herself to exhausted at the end of the day to think about what she was going to do. When she lay down on her hard cot she fell asleep almost immediately.

It was the following week when Lucy asked Beatrice for an errand that fate stepped in.

"Sam, where are you?" Lucy's voice called from the kitchen.

"I think he went upstairs," Bea called to her.

"I wouldn't be surprised," Lucy shook her head, "Probably sneakin' another catnap. The man's never around when I need him."

"Is there something I can do?" Bea asked from the door.

"I'm in the middle of making my pies and I ran out of apples. I was hopin' he would go down in the cellar and fetch me some." Lucy sighed.

"I'll get them for you," Bea offered.

"Would you dear?" Lucy looked up over her spectacles waving a floured hand. "Take a candle with you and mind the steps."

The damp fruit cellar was not Beatrice's favorite place. Spider webs hung from the low ceiling and she'd heard the scurry of mice on many occasions when she'd gone down there but, how could she refuse Lucy a favor. The woman worked so hard and had been so kind to her.

With a sigh, Bea took a candle from the shelf and lit it. She set it on the table while she lifted the heavy trap door. She took a deep breath and gingerly stepped on the first rickety step.

Reaching the bottom, she brushed a web from her hair and held the candle high peering into the darkness.

In the flickering light she saw a bushel basket filled with apples in a dark corner. She lifted the corners of her apron, making a pouch, in which She placed all the fruit she could carry. Rustling sounds coming from the corner made her cut her errand short and run for the stairs.

She started up the steps, candle held out before her. Her other hand held a firm grip on the apples in her apron. She was halfway up when she felt something slide across her foot. She let out a shriek and the candle fell from her grasp. In the dark she felt something clinging to her skirts. Fighting panic, she let go of her apron and heard the apples fall. In the dark she brushed at her skirt but in so doing, lost her balance. Her hand reached out frantically for something to hold on to but only found empty space. The next thing she knew she felt herself falling over and over down the stairs.

"Sam, go get Doctor Morris," Lucy cried as she bent over the girl lying still at the bottom of the stairs.

The doctor, who's office was in the next block, returned on the run, clutching his black bag, Sam, panting behind him.

The doctor quickly took in the scene. Bea lay, not moving, on the dirt floor of the cellar with one leg bent under her but what alarmed him most was the blood forming a puddle around her.

"Bea, can you hear me?" he asked, patting her cheek gently.

His answer was a small moan as pain contorted her face.

"Sam give me a hand," he called up the stairs, "She's hurt bad. We've got to get her to the hospital."

Several hours later when Beatrice opened her eyes she was startled to find herself in a high bed in room with strange smells. Gazing around the room she saw a woman with a white cap standing next to the bed.

"Where am I?" she managed to say through dry lips.

"Lay still, dear," the nurse said. gentle fingers probing her wrist. "You're in Women's hospital."

"But how?" Beatrice asked, trying to rise. A sharp pain in her head made her drop back unto the pillow.

"Please don't try to move. I'll go get Doctor Morris," the woman said going out the door.

Beatrice closed her eyes and lay still as memories of falling into the dark cellar came back to her.

"How are you feeling, Bea?" Doctor John's voice, close to the bed, startled her.

"I hurt all over, especially my leg." she managed to answer him.

"I'm not surprised. That was quite a spill you took," he said, taking her hand in his, "You broke your ankle when you fell."

"Oh, dear!" Beatrice bit her lip, "How will I be able to work?"

"Bea, there is something else," The doctor's kindly eyes probed hers. "I'm afraid you lost the child you were carrying."

Flushing with embarrassment, she turned away, unable to meet his steady gaze.

"Is that why you ran away?" He asked quietly, "To hide this from your family?"

"No, no, you don't understand," she turned to face him, angry that he would think her a wanton woman. "I ran away from my husband. I didn't know I was with child."

"Do you want me to find him and tell him what happened?" he asked gently.

"NO! You musn't!" she gripped his hand, "He'll be so angry. He might—"

"Surely he will forgive you."

"Forgive me? You don't know Jed." she moaned. "If he found out I lost his child, he would—kill me."

"Try not to worry about it now," The doctor said trying to calm her. "You need to rest."

"Promise you won't try to find him?" she implored, tears glistening on her cheeks.

"I promise," he assured her. The doctor stared down at the terrified girl. What kind of a man would harm her?

"You're looking much better today," Doctor John stood at the foot of her bed smiling. Beatrice had been in the hospital for over a week.

"Nurse Wilkes helped me out of bed this morning," she told him," She's teaching me how to use a crutch."

"When you get used to it, you will be able to leave."

"Leave the hospital?" Her face paled as she shrank back into the pillows. "I don't know if I can go back to Lucy's."

"That's what I came to talk to you about," The doctor said, pulling up a chair. "Although I'm sure Lucy and Sam would be happy to take you back, I don't think you're up to working for a while. So I've made arrangements for you to stay at Mrs. Collin's boarding house until you are feeling better."

"That's very kind but I don't have much money," Beatrice began.

"She owes me a favor and I told her when you felt better you could help her in the kitchen for your board."

"That would be wonderful," Beatrice said, tears forming in her blue eyes. "I don't know how to thank you."

"There is something else I have to tell you." the doctor looked solemnly at her.

"It's not my husband?" she drew back in fear, "He's not coming is he?"

"No, no I haven't tried to contact him," the doctor took her hand in his. "When you fell, you lost a lot of blood and I had to operate to stop it." His voice softened to a whisper as he looked into her troubled eyes, "I'm afraid you will never be able to have any more children."

Beatrice stared at him trying to comprehend what he was saying. She could never have children? She closed her eyes and turned to the wall.

"I'm so sorry," she heard the doctor's voice, "I'll leave you alone for a while."

She heard his footsteps and the swoosh of the door. Glad he was gone. She could not let him see the relief on her face, lest it betray her. It wouldn't matter if Jed knew where she was, now. He wouldn't want her. All he'd ever cared about was an heir. She pulled the pillow to her mouth to hide her smile. The thought of having children had always frightened her. Now, she would never have to worry about it again.

CHAPTER TWENTY-SIX

"Someone's comin'" Bernadette called out from the porch.

Jenny peered out the kitchen window wondering who it might be. Judging from the way the horse and buggy was flying down the road, they were in a big hurry. Drying her hands on her apron, she stood in the open door to await their visitor, Emma on her hip. Clayton and Earl peered out from behind her skirts with curiosity.

As it drew near, she recognized the Farnsworth's rig. For a moment her heart lifted. Maybe, Beatrice had come back. Soon, however, she saw it was only the two Farnsworth men. They pulled into the yard in a cloud of dust. What ever they wanted, could only be more trouble.

"Where's your husband?" The elder Farnsworth snarled as he stomped across the yard.

"He's in the barn." Jenny answered him coldly. "What is it?"

"I want to show him what that daughter of yours has gone and done, now." he said waving some papers in his hand.

"What would that be?" Levi asked rounding the corner of the house, his face set in harsh lines. He'd seen them coming down the road.

"She got herself a lawyer and sent my son divorce papers," The elder Farnsworth's face was red with rage. "Divorce?" Levi frowned in disbelief.

"That's right," He said, shaking the papers in Levi's face, "If anybody should be gettin' a divorce it's Jed here." he pointed to his son standing by the rig with a knowing smile on his face.

"If he'd a treated her right, she wouldn't of run off," Levi's voice was cold.

"Well, you can just tell that uppity girl of yours we got ourselves a lawyer too, and Jed is getting his own divorce," Farnsworth said shoving the papers at Levi.

"That's up to you," Levi's voice was hardly above a whisper. "We haven't heard from the girl since she left."

"*If,* you hear from her, you can tell your daughter Jed don't want no more to do with the likes of her."

"Suit yourself," Levi said turning his back and heading toward the field.

"Who'd want to be married to a barren woman anyway," Jed's sneering voice carried across the yard.

Jenny brought her hand to her mouth with a gasp. Levi turned and stared at the man.

"That's what she said in the letter she writ. She can't have any children." Jed smirked with the news that shocked Beatrice's parents. "Always knew somethin' was wrong with her. Who'd want her now?" He called out as he climbed up in the buggy. With a clatter of hoofs they were gone. "Do you think it's true?" Jenny hurried after Levi.

"Don't matter none," he said, not slowing his step. "After what she's done, bringing disgrace to our family."

"But Levi, she's our daughter!" Jenny cried.

"Not anymore." he turned to face his wife, "I never want her name mentioned in our house again!"

Jenny stood twisting her apron in her hands staring at her husband.

"You understand, woman? Never say her name again!" he said, turning his back and striding back to the fields.

Beatrice's parents might have been upset by her actions but as she hummed to herself in Mrs. Collins bright kitchen, she was the happiest she could ever remember. She loved her tiny room upstairs. It was the first time she'd ever had a place to herself and she truly enjoyed the privacy of it.

Her relationship with Doctor John had blossomed. She'd told

him, tearfully, how her husband had beaten and abused her. If she'd exaggerated a little, what was the harm? John had been so kind and understanding, even arranged for her to see a divorce lawyer.

Beatrice's ankle had nearly mended as the Christmas holidays approached and she found helping Mrs. Collins, her motherly landlady a pleasant task. The woman had shown her how to use her new White treadle sewing machine and to her surprise, Beatrice found she was quite adept at it. Seeing the good job she was doing, some of the other borders paid her to do small jobs for them. A hem here or a pocket repaired brought her enough money to do some shopping for herself. She became a regular at the dry goods store.

A few weeks before Christmas she had found a real bargain, a remnant of dark blue velvet was on sale at half price. It had some faint water stains but with careful cutting she knew she could make herself a new dress. She couldn't wait to get back to the boarding house and start sewing.

The morning before Christmas she helped Mrs. Collins finish baking pies and cookies for the holiday. By noon they were done and she hurried to her room to put on her new dress. It had turned out better than she had hoped. The high neck was set off with a white lace collar. The pearl buttons she found in a button box, ran down the front of the bodice to her tiny waist. She spun around in front of Mrs. Collins full length mirror and was pleased with the sight. Now, she awaited Doctor John.

They were going to his sister's for Christmas eve. She didn't know how much John had told them but Edith and Henri had been very kind and had welcomed her on many occasions. "What time is Doctor Morris picking you up?"

"He should be here soon."

"Before he gets here, I have a little something for you." Mrs. Collins said, reaching into the hall closet.

"This is for you," She said, bringing out a long blue woolen cape with a hood lined in white satin. She held it out to her.

"For me? Beatrice asked taking the cloak. "Wherever did you get it?"

"One of my tenants left it here years ago and it being a mite small for me, I could never wear it."

"Oh." Beatrice bit her tongue at the faint odor of mothballs. "It's very nice." she told the smiling landlady. In truth, she hated wearing hand-me-downs but lifted her chin and smiled as Mrs. Collins placed it around her shoulders. She had to admit grudgingly, it was warmer than her thin coat. She'd wear it this winter but another year she vowed, she'd have a new cloak of her own.

The doctor soon arrived. He stood inside the door staring appreciatively. She'd pulled her thick auburn hair up from her delicate neck, letting a single ringlet fall down her cheek. The blue velvet gown set off her flawless complexion and brought out the deep blue of her eyes.

"You look very nice, Bea." was all he managed to say but she had seen the look in his eyes and was very pleased with herself. Beatrice and Doctor John were warmly welcomed at his sister's home. The big house was decorated with huge wreath of holly on the door. Inside, the warmth and smell of pine coming from garlands entwined up the banisters with red ribbons mixed with tantalizing odors coming from the kitchen was almost overwhelming.

Edith hugged them warmly and took their coats. Leading them to the living room where Henri resplendent in a velvet smoking jacket and a red silk vest rose to greet them. "Merry Christmas John, Bea," he took their hands in his and brought Bea's to his lips in his usual greeting.

Beatrice gazed with awe at the ten foot tree in the corner. It was covered with shiny balls and ropes of beads with a shimmering angel on the top. It was breathtaking. She smiled at her hosts and joined them in a glass of eggnog before the crackling fireplace.

They soon sat down to a magnificent dinner of sweet sugared ham and roasted turkey with all the trimmings. Beatrice valiantly tried to do justice to the huge meal but had to decline the Cherry torte with whipped cream served for desert. Not John and young Phillipe, however, who asked for seconds.

After dinner they returned to the livingroom where Edith played carols on the grand piano. They all joined in singing *Oh Come all ye faithful* and *It came upon a Midnight clear*. It was when they began to sing *Silent Night* that Bea suddenly felt sad. John, whose arm was around her shoulders, felt her tense. "Are you all right?" he whispered.

"I'm fine. It just reminds me of when I was a little girl." she said. Although she joined in the others as they sang, the bittersweet memory of Papa lifting her up to the tree and holding her while they sang saddened her.

"Believe it's time for you to say goodnight, Phillipe," his father said as they boy tried to hide a yawn.

"But Papa, I want to wait for Santa Claus." he argued.

"He will not come until you are asleep," Edith said, picking up the boy. "Say goodnight to Uncle John and Miss Bea."

With a promise from his parents that they would set cookies out for Santa, the boy reluctantly agreed to go to bed.

The evening had gone by quickly and soon it was time for them to leave.

Bea thanked them for their hospitality and they wished each other happy holidays.

John tucked a warm blanket around Bea and they set off for home. The air was crisp and clear and the stars shone brightly as the rode along, bells on the horse's reins jingling in the night. "Are you cold?"

"Just a little," Beatrice admitted. "Is this better?" he asked putting his arm around her and pulling her close.

"Much better," she said, smiling to herself. They rode along in pleasant silence.

"Bea?" his voice was soft in her ear.

"Yes, John," she looked up trying to see his face in the moonlight.

"Bea," he swallowed and began again, "I know we haven't known each other very long."

"But John, I feel as though I've always known you," Beatrice said, snuggling closer to him.

"Whoa," he called out, bringing the horse to a stop.

"What's wrong?" She sat up, startled.

"Nothing's wrong, my dear," he said turning to her, taking her hands in his he searched her face in the pale moonlight.

"Bea, do you know how much I've come to love you?"

"Oh, John, after all you know about me, how can you?" She whispered, tears glistening on her eyelashes.

"My darling, you are the most beautiful, courageous woman I've ever met." he said, taking her face gently in his big hands, "Do you think you could learn to love me?"

"John, I must confess. I have loved you from the beginning, even though I knew it was wrong when I was married to Jed," she said bowing her head. With gentle hands he lifted her face, kissing her eyelids, cheeks and then her trembling lips.

Beatrice had trouble returning his kiss with controlled passion. She had dreamed of the moment for so long it was difficult not to respond with abandon.

After a time, he pulled away, fumbling in his coat pocket, "I have something for you."

She watched in fascination as he opened a small box and took out a ring that twinkled in the light from the buggy's lantern.

"I want to take care of you the rest of your life." His voice was heavy with emotion, "Will you marry me, Bea?"

"If you'll have me," she said touching his face and finding tears there also.

"You've made me the happiest man in the world!" he said, placing the sparkling diamond on her finger and pulling her to him. This time she did not hold back the passion.

CHAPTER TWENTY-SEVEN

Jennie snapped the reins and old Dobbin picked up his gait a bit. She was on her way to her sister Dehlia's for a quilting party. It was a brisk March day and she was looking forward to an afternoon with the ladies.

It had been a long cold winter and the hint of spring in the air was invigorating. She smiled down at her two daughters sitting beside her. Bernadette, her chubby little six year old, kept her arm protectively around her younger sister, Emma.

Jenny's thoughts went to her family. They were all growing up so fast. Homer and Roy had moved to Escanaba to work. It was a busy port on Lake Michigan and lots of jobs were available, or so they told her when they left.

Carl and Abner had worked all winter in the lumber camps and would probably be leaving home soon. Cheerful Carl, always smiling. How she would miss him!

A frown crossed her brow as she thought of her eldest daughter, Beatrice. She wondered if Levi would ever forgive her. Secretly, she didn't blame her for leaving Jed Farnsworth. No woman should have to put up with his abuse but to divorce him and marry someone else was unheard of. Jenny sighed. In spite of everything, she hoped her daughter had married a good man this time and found some happiness.

"Will we get there soon?" Bernadette asked, tugging at her mother's sleeve. "Emma has to go potty."

"It's just over the next hill," Jenny assured her, "She can wait."

"Go potty!" the little girl insisted.

"Come sit on my lap," Jenny offered, "You can help me watch for Grandma's barn."

Distracted, Emma crawled up onto her mother's knees. Jenny rested her chin on the child's head and breathed in the scent of her youngest. She'd always tried not to show favoritism with her children but Emma was such a beautiful child. Her golden curls hung down from her bonnet and long matching lashes accented her cornflower blue eyes. Her sweet smile had endured her to all, making slaves of her older brothers.

Jenny's mind again drifted as they bounced along in silence. She wondered if Emma was her last. The child had turned three last month. Maybe it was just as well. Although she did her best to hide it, Jenny had not been well for some time. The wracking cough she got each winter had been especially bad this year. She shook away the worries. It was a lovely spring day and she would feel better when the warm weather came. As promised, when they reached the top of the next hill the old LaBlanc farm came into view. Since Dehlia and her husband Marcel had moved in with Mrs. LaBlanc the farm had not been kept up like it had been when her father was alive. Some of the fences needed mending and the barn he and her brother had built needed paint. She'd mention it to Levi. Maybe he could find time to help Marcel.

Jenny pulled into the barnyard and noted several other rigs already there. The girls jumped down and headed for the outhouse while she tied Dobin's reins.

The smell of warm baked goods greeted them when they entered the kitchen.

"Come in, come in." her mother gestured, ushering them in the door. "The ladies are all in the parlor." She said, taking Jenny's shawl. "I don't suppose you girls would like a treat." she said, as she led the eager children to the cookie jar.

Jenny looked around the room and smiled at the familiar faces. Trudy and Irma, her old school chums came to give her hugs. Dehlia sat at the oak table with Mary and Elizabeth Springer working on a large patchwork quilt. Jenny joined them and they all began chatting, catching up on local gossip, as their fingers flew over the stitches.

"Hear tell, Jane Burns is expecting again," Trudy volunteered as she threaded her needle. "Will that make nine or ten?" her sister Irma asked.

"Only nine," Dehlia spoke up. "She's got a long way to go to top my sister's eleven."

"She's still young," Jenny said quickly noting the bitterness in Dehlia's voice. Dehlia had never been able to carry a baby to full term, resulting in several miscarriages and it was a great disappointment to her.

The women gossiped and worked on the quilt for some time until Mrs. LaBlanc announced coffee was ready. The women put down their needles and followed her to the kitchen where a table laden with warm biscuits and jam awaited.

"Before we start, I have a new game to play." Dehlia announced when all the women were seated. They turned to see her standing with a tin of saltines.

"You have to eat a cracker and then whistle a tune." she told them as she passed them around. "It's such fun and the first one who can do it gets a prize."

The women shrugged and each took a wafer from her. Trudy was the first. She puckered up and they all laughed as the crumbs flew from her mouth. Irma didn't have much luck either and the women were all giggling at each other's attempts.

No one noticed Jenny's face turning red until Dehlia called out. "Sister? Are you all right?" Jenny sat clutching her throat, her eyes wide in panic. She had inhaled the dry crumbs into her windpipe and was choking. The women patted her on the back. Mrs. LaBlanc tried in vain to force water into her mouth but to their horror, in a few minutes she slumped in her chair and stopped breathing.

The women sat stunned. No one could believe it. Josephine cradled her daughter's head in her arms moaning, "Non, Non," as tears ran down her wrinkled cheeks.

"What's wrong with Mamma?" Bernadette's voice called from the door.

"She's sick," Dehlia said, hurrying the child outside. "Lets go find uncle Marcel. He'll go for your Papa."

The women gently lifted Jenny's still body and carried it to her mother's room, laying her on the bed. She looked so peaceful. Her auburn hair, touched with grey now, spread over the pillow. When they closed her eyes and it was as if she was sleeping. It was hard to comprehend she was really gone. Quietly they withdrew and left Josephine to mourn her oldest daughter.

When they heard Levi's rig in the yard, the weeping women shrank back in the corner of the parlor, frightened at what he might say of do. He had a reputation for violence. They needn't have worried. He strode past them unseeing, heading for the bedroom. Josephine's quiet voice could be heard and then she stepped out of the room, shutting the door. There was only one sound from the room. The women described it later as a low moan, not unlike a wounded animal. It sent chills down the back of all who heard it. Then it was quiet.

Later, when the door opened, Levi, his face inscrutable, carried his wife's body out of the house, to the wagon. Without a word to anyone, he laid her across the seat. Cradling Jenny's head in his lap, he urged old Dobin to take them home.

CHAPTER TWENTY-EIGHT

Beatrice dabbed at her eyes with a linen handkerchief. Mamma was gone. Waves of regret swept over her. Why hadn't she gone home to see her since she and John had married? It had been almost two years. Papa, of course. She hadn't wanted to face him, but now she'd never look into those kind brown eyes again. It was to late. A sob shook her thin frame.

She stared, unseeing, out the windows of the train as new tears rolled down her cheeks and thought about the funeral. The church had been full. Jenny had been well loved by everyone and people had come from all over Cheyboygan County to pay their respects. A long procession had driven out to the cemetery in Wolverine.

Beatrice had hardly recognized her brothers. Homer was already losing his hair and Roy was so tall and handsome. Poor Carl, seemed to be taking it the hardest, unable to stop his tears. He had always been Mamma's favorite. The younger children seemed so sad and bewildered

Blanche, almost grown at fourteen would have to take care of them now. Beatrice wondered how she would manage.

"Beaty?" a small voice broke into Beatrice's thoughts. "I'm hungry."

"Would you like one of Grandma's cookies?" Beatrice asked, reaching into her bag. The little girl took the sugar wafer and munched contentedly.

Looking down at her youngest sister on the seat beside her, Beatrice felt an emotion she couldn't quite comprehend. It was more than just love. She truly loved John, her kind, gentle husband but this was different. As she looked at the perfect little face framed by golden curls it was almost maternal. Maybe that was it. Emma was the child she could never have.

"Is Mamma coming too?" the little girl looked up. Her deep blue eyes staring into Beatrice's.

"No. Don't you remember? Mamma's gone to heaven, "She put her arm around the little girl hugging her close. "You're going to live with John and I."

"Has Papa gone to heaven too?"

"No, Papa is at home with Bernadette and the others." Beatrice took the little girl on her lap. "Look out the window at the cows." She said, pointing at the farms as they chugged past.

Papa! She tried not to think about what he would say when he realized she'd taken Emma. At the funeral he'd been oblivious to everyone. His sorrow so deep, no one could reach him. She was sure he'd not even known she was there. When the shock wore off, however, she was sure she would have to deal with him.

"Mamma, you've got to speak to Levi," Dehlia looked hopefully at her mother sipping coffee across the table.

"I know it's not easy taking on more children," Josephine agreed, "But the poor little mites have no where else to go."

"When Jenny died I didn't mind taking in Bernadette and little Earl to help out," Dehlia sighed, "But now that Blanche took off to find Carl and Abner it leaves Victor and Clayton alone."

"Maybe Levi can look after them," Josephine said hopefully.

"He can't even take care of himself," Dehlia snorted. "I heard tell he tried to give Victor away to the Farley's. It's been almost two years since Jenny died and I know how he's still grieving but the man don't care nothin' for his family anymore."

"Levi's a good man and he'll come around one day," Josephine tried to assure her. "Meanwhile, winter's coming on and I wouldn't feel right, not knowing if the boys were being fed proper."

"Well, you better try talking to Levi about giving us some

money," Dehlia insisted, "Marcel says we can't afford to take on no more children."

Josephine took a swallow of coffee, not wanting to blurt out what she thought of her son-in-law, Marcel. A lazier man she'd never seen, spending the little money they had on drink and playing cards in Afton. But Dehlia was right about one thing, It was Levi's responsibility to help out with his children's upbringing. She would speak to him.

It was nearly a week later when Levi showed up at the LaBlanc farm with Victor and Clayton in tow.

"Come in, come in," Josephine welcomed the forlorn little boys with a hug. "Would you like some ginger cookies?"

The boy's faces lit up with anticipation. Holding out a fat cookie jar, she noted the holes in their pants and the bedraggled look of them and her heart went out.

"Sit down Levi and have some coffee," Josephine said bustling about, filling a mug from the pot on the stove.

"What brings you this way?" Dehlia asked, hands on hips from the doorway.

"Papa!" Bernadette, carrying Earl, ran to her father. "Have you come to take us home?"

Levi patted the girl absently on the shoulder, "Not just yet," he muttered. "Run along and play with your brothers." Bernadette looked at her father's solemn face and reluctantly coaxed Victor and Clayton outside.

"Miz LaBlanc, I want to thank you, Dehlia and Marcel for takin' in Bernadette and Earl and I want to make it right with you."

"There's no need," Josephine protested, ignoring the look on Dehlia's face. "It's the least we can do for Jenny until you get straightened around."

"What I came to tell you," he took a big swallow from the mug. "I've sold the farm."

"Why Levi, wherever will you go?" Mrs. LaBlanc asked, stunned by his news.

"Thought I'd go up to Cheboygan and sign on with one of them big boats and head down Detroit way." he said quietly.

"What about your children?" Dehlia asked warily.

"I was comin' to that," he said leveling his gaze at her. "I thought maybe I could leave 'em with you and Marcel for the winter."

"Levi, I don't think we can take on any more." Dehlia said shaking her head.

"I'll make it right with you," Levi protested, pulling out his wallet.

"I don't know what Marcel will say, "Dehlia hesitated but her eyes lit up at the bills he lay on the table.

"If you'd do me this favor, I won't forget it." Levi urged, pushing the money toward her.

"Of course we'll take the boys in," Mrs. LaBlanc answered for her. After all, the farm still belonged to her and she had some say in who lived there.

"I'd be much obliged," Levi said rising, "I'll be going now."

"Levi, take care of yourself," Mrs. LaBlanc said, reaching out to him but he backed away, hat in hand.

He nodded to both women and they watched as he stiffly said goodbye to his children and drove out of the yard. Although he sent money on a regular basis, it would be many years before they saw him again.

CHAPTER TWENTY-NINE

(Ten years later 1923)

Beatrice, in a blue satin dressing gown, sat at her dining-room table pouring coffee from a silver pot. Morning sun shown through the french doors making patterns on the oriental rug. John reading the morning paper, at the other end, glanced up and smiled.

"Looks like spring is finally here." he mused noting the tiny buds on the lilac bush growing beside the door. "What are your plans for the day, dear?"

"I'm having lunch with Edith at the Tea Room and then I'm meeting Emma at the dressmakers."

"I'm not wearing that ugly pink thing to the prom," Emma announced, flouncing into the dining room in her usual flurry.

"But Emma, the dress has already been chosen," Beatrice insisted. "We picked it out last week."

"No, you picked it out," Emma frowned at her sister, "You should see it, John," the girl's expression changed as she turned pleading eyes to her brother-in-law. "Its all ruffles and bows and it makes me look like a baby."

"It's a copy of the dress Mary Pickford wears in her new movie," Beatrice insisted.

"Why don't you have several dresses made and you can choose the one you like best." John suggested.

"That's a great idea," Emma beamed at him with just a hint of triumph as she munched her toast.

Beatrice looked across the table at her husband and sighed. John spoiled the girl. She had to admit, however, they both gave in to her whims most of the time.

"Must be off," John announced. Patting Emma's golden curls affectionately as he passed her chair, "Have a good day princess." He stopped to kiss his wife's cheek. "Board meeting this morning and I may be late for dinner, I'll let you know."

Beatrice saw him to the door and stood watching as he got into his new Oldsmobile and waved as he drove out the circular drive. He was head of the hospital now and while she was glad he seldom was called out at night, it seemed to take more and more of his time.

As she was about to close the door she noticed the postman coming and waited for him. He tipped his hat and handed her several letters.

Beatrice returned to the table and absently lay the mail next to her coffee.

"You'd better hurry, Emma." she said, pointing to the grandfather's clock, "You'll be late for school."

"No I won't. Freddy's picking me up in his new Ford roadster." At the sound of a horn, the girl jumped up. "I didn't know Freddy could drive," Beatrice frowned.

"He learned last summer and his Dad bought him a car for his birthday." Emma turned one of her dazzling smiles on her sister as she ran out of the room. "He's a real good driver, Beatty."

"Don't forget to meet me at the dressmakers at four," she called after the girl.

With a sigh, she poured herself another cup of coffee and tried not to worry. Emma, at fifteen was such a beautiful child and growing up so fast. Freddy wasn't the only boy that called.

Beatrice glanced at the mail. A bill from the florist, an invitation to a luncheon at the library, nothing important. Then she saw it. A small envelope carefully addressed in cramped handwriting. She frowned when she noted the Wolverine post mark and slit it open.

With unbelieving eyes she read the terse note from Levi.

> *Dear daughter, Beatrice,*
> *I have moved back to my place in Wolverine. It is my wish that Emma come and live with me. She has been with you long enough. Send her on the next train.*
>
> *Your father,*
> *Levi Wakeford*

Beatrice sat staring at the letter with unbelieving eyes, unaware that her coffee cup had slipped from her hand and oblivious to the dark stain that flowed across the white linen table cloth.

"Mrs. Morris! Are you all right?"

"What?" Beatrice looked up, her head spinning, to see Cora, her housekeeper, standing before her.

"Thank goodness, you came around!" the woman said, nervously twisting her apron. "Shall I send for Doctor Morris?"

"No, no.," Beatrice waved her away as she tried to clear her head. "I'll be fine."

"Are you sure you're all right? You're white as a ghost." the housekeeper insisted.

"It's nothing," Beatrice assured her, rising unsteadily. "See if you can clean this up." she said, pointed to the spilled coffee. Gathering up the strewn mail, she turned and left the room, trying not to show how her legs were shaking.

Once in her own sitting room, she collapsed on her satin chaise lounge, letting the enormity of her father's letter sink in.

How dare her father think he could come back into their lives after all these years!

No one knew where Levi spent his time. She'd heard he'd occasionally dropped in to see Roy or Homer in Wisconsin for a short visit and then be gone again. Beatrice had not seen or heard from him since Mamma died.

Beatrice frowned. Now that she thought of it, she remembered Carl telling her Levi had bought the old Henley cabin in Wolverine last fall. It had been there since she was a child. It couldn't be more that a shack.

She thought of her little sister with the golden curls happily planning her first prom. There was no way the child could go back to live with her father in a place like that.

Beatrice sat up. She would go see Levi, talk to him after all these years. Surely he would see all the advantages she was able to give Emma that he could not. He'd understand.

John had a medical convention in Chicago the coming weekend and Beatrice decided not to mention her father's letter to John. Instead, she checked train schedules and found one left for Wolverine at seven Friday night.

Emma was spending the weekend with one of her girl friends and it would be a perfect time for her to go.

She would arrive Saturday morning, have a talk with Levi and be back on the afternoon train. No one would even know she'd been gone.

CHAPTER THIRTY

There was a slight chill and a hint of rain as Beatrice made her way across the nearly deserted platform of the Pontiac train station. She pulled her loose fitting coat tightly around her and climbed the steps to the waiting car.

She breathed a small sigh of relief as the train pulled out of the station. There were only a few passengers in the car. A heavy woman with a cranky child, an elderly man sitting stiffly with his satchel held firmly on his knees and a young couple holding hands. No one had noticed her. It wouldn't do to have met one of her or John's friends and have to explain where she was going at this time of night.

She pulled off her cloche hat and ran her fingers through her newly bobbed hair. It felt so strange after all these years of wearing it long but she liked the feel of it.

Beatrice learned back against the plush seat and closed her eyes feeling the gentle sway of the train. It brought back memories of other trips she had made. Her tearful trip home from her Aunt Marie's with her father when she was just a child. The long, miserable trip to Idaho and back. Later, when she had escaped from Jed and the last trip when Mamma had died. All of them had been worrisome but this was the worst of all.

Her father's stern face swam before her closed eyes. She'd always been a little afraid of him, but he was an old man now, over sixty. Perhaps he'd mellowed.

Whether the years had changed him or not she would try to reason with him. He shouldn't be living alone in an old drafty cabin. Thinking Emma would want to stay there with him would be out of the question. If all else failed, she would consider asking him to come and live with her and John.

One thing for sure, she would not let him make a slave out of her sister as he had mamma. A tear ran down her cheek as she thought of her mother. All those years of hardship. Carrying water from the river to wash clothes, Digging in the hard, unyielding, ground to plant a garden. Through it all, never complaining, she'd taken care of everyone. Beatrice wished with all her heart that she could have done something to make her mother's life easier.

Her own childhood came back to her. Being the oldest girl she'd had the burden of looking out for her younger siblings. All the running noses she'd wiped. How many flour sack diapers had she changed or when they got older, taking them on trips to the outhouse. It seemed all of her childhood was spent looking after them. It was probably the reason she didn't regret her inability to have any of her own.

All of her brothers and sisters were grown now and several had married. Carl, the only one with children had moved to Detroit recently with his pretty wife Nellie and a son and daughter.

The rest were scattered between Escanaba and Racine, except for Abner. What a pesky child he had been. Always teasing her. At seventeen, he was the only brother to join the Army. She wondered if the discipline had changed him. The last she'd heard after the war he'd gone to California and was working for some man named Griffith.

Beatrice dozed as the train made it's way past Bay City and continued North. The eastern sky was just starting to lighten when the train pulled into Wolverine.

Pulling on her hat, which covered most of her face, Beatrice stepped down from the train. The old station looked the same. She sighed and took a deep breath. The damp morning air stung her chest and brought on a choking spell. She would have to ask John for more cough medicine. He'd been nagging her to come in to the hospital for a check up for some time. Thoughts of her mother's chronic cough came back in startling clarity. Much as she hated the idea, she would go in when she got back. Holding a linen handkerchief to her mouth she hurried across the platform and down the path that led to the Afton road.

Glancing up at the dark clouds to the West threatening more rain she pulled her coat tightly around her and began climbing the road that led to Levi's cabin.

Just past the bridge over the swirling Sturgeon river she found a path. She hoped it would lead to the cabin. Beatrice plunged into the woods unmindful of the early budding Oaks or the Trailing Arbutus flowers she crushed beneath her feet.

She smelled smoke before she actually saw it coming from the cabin's chimney and knew she was almost there.

Just short of the wooden steps, she stopped to catch her breath. Ignoring the sharp pain in her chest she climbed onto the flimsy porch and knocked sharply on the door. It opened slowly.

"It's you!" he said, opening the door. His lips curled in distaste, "Where's Emma?"

"I didn't bring her," Beatrice stared back at her father. The years had not been kind. His hair was white now. Papery thin skin stretched across his hollow cheeks. Only those piercing blue eyes remained the same and they stared angrily at her.

"Can I come in, Papa?"

Levi turned away but left the door open.

Beatrice followed him into the tiny Cabin taking in its meager furnishings. A bowl and spoon sat on the table covered with worn blue oil cloth.

Against the far wall sat a neatly made iron cot with a patchwork quilt. Levi turned to the black cook stove. Sparks flew as he put a small piece of kindling in the grate.

"Why didn't you bring the girl?" Levi asked in a raspy voice, still not turning to face her.

"Papa," Beatrice hesitated, not knowing how to begin,. "Emma is so happy with John and I. We were hoping you'd understand and let her stay with us."

"Teaching her all your high faluting city ways, are you?" Levi turned to face her.

"No, you don't understand," Beatrice swallowed trying to keep her rising temper under control. "She's doing so well in school and she has so many friends. She wouldn't be happy away from everyone she grew up with."

"Afton school was good enough for you," he muttered. Pulling out a chair from the table, he sat down, his back rigid.

Beatrice, trying to control her shaking knees, Looked around. She saw the only other place to sit was the cot. Gingerly she perched on the edge. Taking off her hat, she ran her fingers through her hair.

"Shaved your head like some Harlot, I see."

His words spoke venom. "Don't think I'm going to let you teach Emma all your evil ways!"

Ignoring his words, Beatrice gestured around the bare cabin. "You don't even have a place for her to sleep."

Levi sat stubbornly staring into space.

"Would you like some coffee, Papa?" Beatrice asked, noting the pot bubbling on the stove next to an iron skillet.

"Mind you don't spill it." he growled.

With a sigh, she took two mugs from the shelf and filled them from the metal pot.

Beatrice set the coffee before her father and welcomed the warm liquid as she sipped from her own cracked cup.

"This is no place for Emma, or you either Papa," she began, "Why don't you come back to Pontiac and stay with John and I."

"Live in a house of sin? Never!" Levi banged his mug on the table. Rivulets of steaming brown liquid ran across the cracked oil cloth.

"What are you talking about?" Two spots of color had arisen in her pale cheeks.

"You left your husband to go with another man." his accusing voice echoed through the cabin. "God will punish you for your sins!"

"You think I should have stayed with that drunken brute, Jed?" Beatrice stared at her father. "Even If I hadn't met John I couldn't live with those lying Farnsworths."

"You ran off against my wishes and then couldn't stay and be a decent wife." Levi spat his words. "You were always willful. Never could do what was right."

"Papa, that was a long time ago." Beatrice said trying to control her anger. "John and I have been married for years. He is a respected man and kindest I've ever known!"

"What kind of *respected* man seduces another man's wife?" Levi sneered, stubbornly. "He's the devil's own and I'll not let Emma stay with you in his house!"

Beatrice stood quietly behind her father. He could not see the look in her eyes as they slowly turned opaque.

"You bring Emma to me or I'll have the law on you both!" he threatened, his fist pounding the table.

As if it had a mind of it's own, Beatrice's hand reached out and grasped the iron fry pan from the back of the stove. Thinking he had won the argument, Levi half turned. By the time he heard the whoosh, it was too late.

It was some time before Beatrice's eyes again focused. She looked down with a puzzled frown at the heavy skillet still in her hand and set it back on the stove. Then her foot touched something soft and she stared with horror at Levi's still form at her feet. Backing away, she stumbled backward to the cot. Grabbing her hat and bag she fled from the cabin. Reaching the porch, her knees threatened to give out and slowly she lowered herself to the steps.

Rocking back and forth, she tried to get her breath. What had she done!

Staggering to her feet, she lurched down the path. She had to get away! No one must know! She must get back to Emma and John!

Branches tore at her clothes as she ran hysterically through the woods, unaware of the cold spring rain soaking her clothes. By the time she had reached the road she was exhausted and a coughing spell forced her to slow her pace. She approached the bridge and steadied herself against the iron railing. From this vantage point she could look down at the town of Wolverine. She breathed a sigh of relief when she saw the train from Cheyboygan heading into the station on it's return trip South.

Beatrice never knew how she made it down the hill and onto the waiting train, but somehow she found a seat, where she collapsed, staring out the window.

"We're at the Pontiac station, Miss. Are you all right? The conductor stared at the woman in the last row of the car. He had thought her sleeping but upon closer inspection realized she was unconscious. With the help of the station master they carried her into the depot. When they still couldn't rouse her, an ambulance was summoned.

CHAPTER THIRTY-ONE

"Where's my wife?" John stood impatiently at the Nurses station.

"Room fourteen," Nurse Wilkes pointed to the right, "Doctor Blake is with her."

John's long legs took him to the room in two steps. He pulled open the heavy door and stopped, stunned at what he saw. Beatrice lay still, eyes closed, her face was white as the sheet that covered her. The raspy sound of her belabored breathing filled the room. He strode quickly to the bed placing his hand on her forehead, frowning as he felt the heat emanating from her.

"Dr. Morris," Dr. Blake a small grey haired man with wire rimmed glasses removed a thermometer from her parched lips, frowning as he read it. "I'm glad you're here."

"How bad is it?" John asked. Taking his eyes from the still form of his wife, he searched the face of his colleague.

"Her fever's very high," The older Doctor shook his head, "We haven't been able to bring it down. I'm afraid you're wife is in an advanced stage of Double Pneumonia," he said, taking John's arm, "Perhaps we should step outside." "I don't understand." John shook his head as Dr. Blake led him out of the room. "When I left on Friday she said she had a slight cold, but nothing like this. I would never have left her."

"Sometimes these things develop quickly." the doctor shrugged.

"What are her chances?" John searched the other man's face for answers and drew back at the look he found there.

"We've done all we can do," The Doctor sighed, "If her fever breaks by morning, we'll see."

"There must be something else. You've got to save her!" John grabbed the smaller man by the shoulders in desperation.

"You're a Physician, you know how serious Pneumonia can be," Dr. Blake backed away, his eyes full of compassion.
"Yes, of course," John said quietly.

* * *

"John! You're here!" Emma rushed down the corridor and threw herself at her brother-in-law sobbing. "Beatty, she's so sick!"
"I know, I know," John patted the girl awkwardly.
"I didn't know what to do. They sent someone from the hospital and said she was here." Emma raised her young tear stained face, "You were in Chicago and I didn't know how to reach you so I called Doctor Blake."
"You did the right thing," John said trying to smile reassuringly at her.
"I'm so glad you're back," she sighed clinging to his arm, "I know you can help her."
"Of course, of course," He said turning away from the girl, staring at the door to his wife's room. "Why don't you go home for a while and get some rest, Princess?"
"I am pretty tired," Emma sighed, "I've been here all day."
"Run along then," he said, patting her shoulder, "I'll stay with Bea."
John stood by helplessly as the nurses tended his wife. They held a glass to her dry lips trying to get her to swallow. The water ran down her chin. He bathed her face in the cool water they brought in a basin. Nothing helped. Her breathing became more labored and she began to toss and turn. In her delirium she called out to her mother and Emma. Once she became particularly agitated and in a raspy voice cried, "Papa, No!"

"Bea, it's all right," John sat on the edge of the bed. Cradling her in his arms, he soothed her. It seemed to help a little. He bit back tears of anguish as he held her frail body.

It was almost morning when Beatrice opened her eyes. She tried to smile as she recognized the face of her distraught husband.

Raising her small hand, she touched his unshaven cheek. He brought her fingers to his lips. She struggled to speak. John leaned forward to hear her raspy voice.

"Emma, promise you'll take care of her." She gasped. The effort drained her and brought on a wracking cough that seemed to tear her apart.

"Bea, don't try to talk." John held her to him. "You mustn't worry. You know I'll look after Emma."

With a sigh she closed her eyes and was gone.

* * *

Where was he? Levi's eyes focused on the legs of the cook stove. What was he doing on the floor? He pushed himself upright and shook his head. He blinked as he looked around the familiar cabin.

Brushing his hair back from his eyes he winced as he felt the bump on his head. He must have fallen. Slowly the previous events came back to him. Where was Beatrice? She'd must have run off and left him here. Well, good riddance! Who did she think she was, her and her uppity Doctor husband thinking they could keep Emma from him.

Slowly, he got to his feet, holding on to the table for support. He lowered himself onto the wooden chair for a moment until his head stopped reeling.

Beatrice must have gone back to Wolverine to take the train. Levi pulled out his pocket watch and noted it was just past Eight. If he hurried, he could catch it.

A sly smile played around his lips. Wouldn't she be surprised when she found out he was on the train. He would go down to Pontiac and bring Emma home with him and they better not try and stop him!

He rose and heading for the door. He took his jacket and hat from a peg and hurried out. As he stepped out on the porch a sharp pain ran down his arm. *What nonsense was this*, he thought. *Can't be bothered now.* He hurried down the steps determined to catch the train.

A short way down the path it came again.

He tried to steady himself against a tall pine, but found he could not go on. His back against the tree, he slid to the ground and sat there staring into the woods. The pain subsided a little but he found he was too weak to move.

Through the trees he saw someone coming but was found he could not call out. He watched helplessly as the form of a woman approached him. When she got closer she looked like—No! it couldn't be, But It was. His beloved Jenny standing before him.

She stretched out her hand. "It's time, Levi,"

All pain left him as he rose to follow her.